KATHRYN LASKY

WOLVES OF THE BEYOND
STAR WOLF

SCHOLASTIC PRESS / NEW YORK

Library of Congress Cataloging-in-Publication Data
Lasky, Kathryn.
Star wolf / Kathryn Lasky. — 1st ed.
p. cm. — (Wolves of the beyond ; 6)
Summary: The Ring of Sacred Volcanoes has been destroyed and Faolan is
leading his small band of wolves across the Ice Bridge to the hoped-for safety of
the Distant Blue — but his old enemy Heep is pursuing him and the icy path
ahead is filled with danger.
ISBN 978-0-545-54769-7
1. Wolves — Juvenile fiction. 2. Animals — Juvenile fiction. [1. Wolves —
Fiction. 2. Animals — Fiction. 3. Fantasy.] I. Title. II. Series: Lasky, Kathryn.
Wolves of the Beyond ; 6.
PZ7.L3274Su 2013
813.54 — dc23
2012029320

10 9 8 7 6 5 4 3 2 1   13 14 15 16 17

Printed in the U.S.A.   40
First edition, January 2013

Map illustration by Whitney Lyle
Book design by Lillie Howard

A long trek comes to a close —
a journey not possible without my
editor and navigator, Rachel Griffiths

K. L.
Cambridge, MA
October 2012

THE ICE BRIDGE

THE
CRYSTAL
PLAIN
OF THE
BEYOND

Frozen
Sea

CONTENTS

AHHOOOOOO GARROOO!

AS THE SILVER WOLF TOOK HIS first step onto the Ice Bridge, he turned back to look behind him at his final den in the Beyond. He had slept there with fourteen traveling companions, who were straggling out of the den now. Eight fully grown wolves, three wolf pups, two bear cubs, and a Masked Owl. They, too, turned around to take their last look at the only continent they had ever known — that of the Beyond. It was destroyed now. Famine struck the first blow, and then came the earthquakes. Only a very few had survived, and now this motley brigade of fifteen creatures was all that counted in Faolan's mind.

Every one of them was looking longingly in the wrong direction — east. There was nothing to the west save for an endless expanse of white, the Frozen Sea, over which a bridge of ice arced like an inverted crescent moon. Faolan tipped his head one way, then the other. The bridge appeared to be supported by thick ice pillars. Sometimes the bridge rose quite high, and the thought of slipping off it and smashing onto the ice below was terrifying. And sometimes the bridge swooped low, skimming over the dark pools in the Frozen Sea where the ice had broken to expose water.

Faolan wondered how long the bridge had been there. Would there be signs of others who had crossed before — hoofprints? Paw prints? How could anything grow on the bridge? It seemed stark and sterile, incapable of supporting life. But Gwynneth, who had passed a great deal of time with owls in the northern kingdoms, had said that the owls found rodents in the ice — lemmings, snow mice, something called rockmunks, similar to chipmunks. Rodents would sustain owls for a while, but wolves needed more.

The end of the bridge seemed to dissolve into nothingness, as did the far edges of the sea. It was the nothingness, the gleaming nothingness of it all, that was the most unnerving.

Faolan tried to bark a command, but the sound broke in his throat. He only vaguely knew where they were heading — a place across the water where they hoped to find a new land and safety. But the way there, this bridge of ice across a vast nothingness, was uncertain. Would a bridge that glistened like the thinnest slice of the moon even reach the new continent they could see only as a blue haze? Because of its color, they had come to call the new continent the Distant Blue. Might there be ruptures in the bridge? And if so, where would their journey end? The wolves could swim, but wolf pups did not learn until they were almost yearlings, and then only in the placid summer waters of rivers. The bridge was wide here at the start, but suppose it narrowed, or broke? If they were marooned in a melting sea on chunks of ice . . . what then?

But the fear that consumed Faolan's waking and sleeping dreams was losing a young one. The young ones would be the marrow of life on this new continent, their most valuable asset. But there was no choice. They must go ahead, despite the danger. There was no life left for them in the Beyond, and they must proceed on faith. He finally mustered a forceful howl.

"Ahhoooooo garrooo!"

It was the point wolf's call to start the *byrrgis*, a hunting pack. It literally meant "Summon your marrow."

Faolan saw each animal take one last glance behind before stepping onto the Ice Bridge. He could not help but wonder what they were each thinking.

CHAPTER ONE

ICE LEGS

MYRR KEPT HIS EYES TRAINED ON his paws as he followed behind Edme. Faolan had told them not to look back again, not even once. They must pay attention, for the Ice Bridge could be dangerous. They might slip or fall. They must concentrate. Myrr, of course, had no desire to look back. Behind him lay only dreadful memories. He had been weaned in the worst possible way. No, his mother had not been killed. That would have been the second-worst possible way to be torn away from her milk. The worst possible way was to have his mother and father look at him blankly, with horrible vacant eyes staring at him as if he were a rock, a piece of wood, a clump of dried grass, a clot of mud. And then they had both turned and walked away. Myrr shook off the thought and continued to walk forward, right in the footsteps of Edme.

Edme was listening carefully. She didn't need to turn around to hear that Myrr was just behind her. She, like Faolan, was consumed with worry not for what she had left behind, but for the young ones. The pup immediately behind her was the most important thing in her world. When his parents had abandoned him and Edme had picked him up and brought him to the Ring of Sacred Volcanoes, Finbar Fengo had named him Myrrglosch, which meant "bit of a miracle" in the Old Wolf language. And it was a bit of a miracle that he had survived when his parents, gripped by the Skaars madness, had abandoned him.

This madness afflicted many during the worst of the famine. Skaars wolves gave up all hope and embraced despair. It made them blind to their own mates, their pups, and their responsibilities as living wolves. It was a perversion of every code that the wolves had lived by in the Beyond. And it had blinded Myrrglosch's parents.

Edme, who had fought her whole life to survive, never understood the Skaars madness. She, like Faolan, had been a *malcadh*, a cursed wolf born deformed. According to the laws and codes governing the wolves of the Beyond, such pups were cast out of their clans at birth. If they managed to survive, they could rejoin a clan as gnaw wolves, objects of abuse. Their only hope was to succeed in the games known as the *gaddergnaw*. If they won, they would then serve as elite Watch wolves at the Ring of Sacred Volcanoes. It was a noble and honorable duty.

Edme now felt a twinge that was not caused by anxiety over the young ones. A wistfulness had sneaked up on her and suddenly overwhelmed her. Would she never again see the dancing fires of the Ring, the flaming tongues from volcanoes licking the night sky? There was such beauty there, especially during the season of the She-Winds, which seemed to stir the very bowels of the volcanoes. The warm air above the craters' flames buoyed their surveillance leaps, and sometimes she felt she could soar as high as the collier owls that swept above the sparks, scavenging the darkness for the hottest embers — bonk embers they called them. Of course, the wolves' task was to guard against the graymalkins who might skim just above the bubbling cauldron in search of the elusive ember of Hoole.

Edme knew that many of her traveling companions took these first steps onto the Ice Bridge with not just trepidation, but hearts heavy for what they were leaving and would never see again. Still, their lives in the Beyond had been far from perfect. The Whistler, like Faolan and

Edme, had been a gnaw wolf, and unlike them had never advanced to serve at the Ring of Sacred Volcanoes. Caila, the Milk Giver to Dearlea and Mhairie, had been seized by the Skaars dancing illness, then became the mate of a vile wolf, Heep, an outclanner. She had borne him a son, Abban, and when she had finally come to her senses, she had fled, leaving her shame behind. The bear cubs, Burney and Toby, were leaving the bones of their mother. And Gwynneth was leaving not only the wreck of her forge, but the bones of her oldest friend, the Sark of the Slough. And there was no choice. They were all desperate animals.

Beneath her feet, Edme detected a certain slipperiness to which she was not accustomed. She turned around.

"Myrrglosch, dear. See how I am digging my toes in?"

"Yes."

"You must do that, too. Firm grip, you know. We must get our ice legs."

"Yes," he said quietly, and dug his toes in deeper.

"If you like, I could carry you in my mouth."

"No! I'm not a whelping pup," he replied stubbornly.

And this is no whelping den, Edme thought. *Far from it!* She looked ahead at the gleaming bridge. In the distance, she thought she saw a slight ridge. It looked like a bump from where they were, but it would get bigger and steeper the closer they came. *How will we ever get over that?*

Three days after the fifteen creatures had taken those first tentative steps onto the Ice Bridge, a yellow wolf, an outclanner, stood on the edge of the western sea. He pawed the ground nervously and felt his marrow begin to boil. *They were here! She was here! How dare they!* A blind rage began to surge through him.

Heep had discovered the last den of Faolan's brigade, and in it he had teased out Caila's scent and the scent of his son. He had found the odd footprint of Faolan with the swirled marks on it still visible, although the splayed paw had turned during the Great Mending and was no longer askew. He himself was no longer a *malcadh*. For this was the prophecy of good King Hoole, the first of the embered owl kings. The prophecy said that when the ember was released, the time of the Great Mending would come and then twisted limbs would be made straight, missing ears or eyes or tails would grow, broken windpipes would be patched. And so it had happened that within minutes of the earthquake that had destroyed the Ring of Sacred Volcanoes and freed the ember, Heep felt a quickening in the muscles of his rump and his tail began to grow.

Once Heep had been a gnaw wolf of the MacDuncan clan. He was a vicious creature, and he had been declared *crait* and driven from the Beyond to the Outermost by order of the clan chieftain. Heep had risen to power among the lawless outclanner wolves and, during the worst of the famine, had seized upon Caila. Instead of killing her and cannibalizing her body as many outclanners did when tracking Skaars wolves, he had renamed Caila "Aliac" and taken her for his mate. But she had finally come to her senses and escaped with their young pup, Abban.

He squinted now into the darkness. Behind him the first rays of the dawn were tinting the sky, but west it was still dark and forbidding. Had Faolan and his followers really gone out on this Ice Bridge? The tracks seemed to confirm that they had. Heep felt a quiver in his marrow. He lifted his tail higher. He didn't want the others to suspect him of doubts or any trace of uncertainty or fear. His rout had grown; they had picked up half a dozen more wolves. He was their leader — would he lead them out onto this bridge? His two worst enemies were out there. Their scent seemed to taunt him. He felt a savage hunger for their blood and their flesh, and imagined his fangs tearing into their muscle.

The MacDuncan chieftain had declared him *crait*, but it was Faolan who had actually driven Heep from the Beyond. Aliac had become his mate, borne his son, then taken that son and escaped. That was the ultimate insult. It stirred a fury in his blood. Of course he would go right these wrongs. He would go to kill Faolan, reclaim his son, and yes, he would kill Aliac. He nearly spat as he thought of her name. She called herself something else now. Calla or Caila. He couldn't remember.

He would call her dead.

CHAPTER TWO

A SLOW HORROR

WHEN EDME HAD SPIED IT THREE days before, that first slight swelling on the bridge had looked like a bump. But when they'd approached it, they'd seen that it was steep and more like a jagged ice wall. Then there had been another and another. These ridges presented a formidable obstacle to the wolves' traveling speed. They were made by ice that had fractured into long cracks and then filled with water during the summertime, only to be refrozen. The refrozen ice buckled, and the ice on one side built up against the other, forming a pressure ridge. The greater the pressure, the higher the ridge, and these ridges had to be crossed. Flying ahead, Gwynneth could often guide the creatures around them if she found a break in the ridge. But more often than not they had to clamber over the jagged obstacles.

Faolan supposed ridges were better than actual cracks through which they might fall, but the ridges slowed their pace. It was their third day on the bridge, and they had encountered four already. The wind was stiff as the little brigade followed Faolan in a straggly line. He could only hope there would not be too many pressure ridges before their next camp.

The pressure ridges did, however, offer two benefits: First, they seemed to abound with lemmings. So for the time being, finding food was not a problem. Second, the ridges offered some shelter from the wind when they made camp to sleep. Now, as the sun broke behind them, casting a pink radiance over the frozen landscape, the way ahead looked clear. Faolan tipped his head up and caught sight of Gwynneth flying.

"How does it look?" he howled. Gwynneth squinted into the paling sky ahead.

"I . . . I . . ." She hesitated before answering. "I think it looks fairly smooth." Her gizzard clenched slightly.

"Just fairly?" Faolan asked.

"Uh . . ."

There was a blast of wind that cut through the air like a scimitar. Never had Faolan felt such force: It was as if the fur were being peeled from his back. Out of the corner of his eye, he caught a glimpse of a small furry pup staggering against the wind. It was Abban! The wind had pushed him to the rim of the Ice Bridge, where he teetered and clung with all his might. And still his paws were slipping.

Faolan's worst anxiety had caught up with him, and a real, living nightmare was unfolding before his eyes. Faolan tried to claw his way toward Abban, but the wind felt like a boulder crushing against him. A terrible squeal unfurled over the Frozen Sea, searing the air, and the little pup spiraled down toward a dark pool in the ice below the bridge.

"ABBAN!" his mother howled.

Gwynneth hurled herself into a steep banking turn, trying to intercept the falling pup.

Great Glaux. She spied the pup just as he dropped into the dark pool of water.

"He's gone!" Gwynneth shreed. The Masked Owl was so shocked that her own wings began to lock.

You can't go yeep! You can't go yeep! You old fool. Faolan silently cursed his oldest friend. *Not now. But what is she to do?* He felt his own marrow seize up. They stood at the edge of the bridge, locked with fear as they peered down into the channel of water that had been pried open

14

by the sea and widened into a pool. The green water glinted darkly, like a liquid eye in the middle of the ice. A howl withered in Caila's throat. She seemed to be gasping for the air that her drowning son could not breathe. Gwynneth had recovered and was skimming close to the surface, looking for any sign of the pup.

How long can he last underwater? Faolan felt his own lungs squeeze together. He had clamped his mouth shut and forgotten to breathe.

"No, Caila!" he screamed with his first breath as he realized that she was about to leap in. Dearlea and Mhairie must have seen it a second before he did, because they both pounced on her and wrestled her to the ground and held her so she would not leap into the sea after her son. The wind had carried Abban directly into the sea, but it had shifted. If Caila leaped, she would be smashed onto the ice below. From this height, on the steepest section of the bridge, every bone in her body would be broken.

Caila howled in despair. Too much time had passed with Abban under the water. Her pup could not be alive.

Abban could never be sure what had made him take a huge breath as he was falling from the bridge. He thought he had opened his mouth to scream. But instead he had swallowed an immense gulp of air, and now he was tumbling softly through the water. A fierce cold penetrated his fur to touch his skin, and his claws curled up tightly. *My eyeballs are freezing,* he thought. *I cannot shut my eyes. My heart will freeze, and then my blood.*

Since he could not shut his eyes, he opened them wider. It seemed to him that the water was like a new kind of sky, a liquid sky with silvery bubbles instead of clouds. Small fish swam by, silent and ghostly. Next came a strange underwater bird with a bright chunky orange beak. The bird swam up close to him, and Abban reached out and gently touched its clownish face. The bird winked, and Abban wanted to wink back. He was starting to starve for air, but as his lungs pressed in on him, an enormous fish swam up. It had a fearsome-looking sword growing out of one side of its head, but Abban was too desperate for air to be afraid.

He felt something nudge against him, and then he was rising to the surface. His head broke through the water, and there was air!

Air, he thought. *Do I dare . . . or do I care?*

There was a pull on his hackles, and he felt himself lifted out of the water. Gwynneth was carrying him by the fur on his neck, higher and higher, but all he could think was that she was taking him away from the liquid sky into the airy one. *I am soaring, and air is boring!*

The wolves on the bridge had gasped when Gwynneth had suddenly folded her wings tightly against her sides and plunged toward the crack. She wasn't going yeep, she was in the pitch of a kill spiral. Except in this case, she was diving for life and not death. She emerged, and in her claws was a sodden mass. It could have been seaweed, it could have been a fish, but it was not. It was Abban the wolf pup, son of Caila.

CHAPTER THREE

Go Forth!

"ABBAN!" CAILA BARKED AS Gwynneth set the pup down at her paws. He looked up at her, shivering so hard it seemed as if his limbs might shake loose. Water dripped from him, and he appeared half his size, for his fur was plastered to his body. He hardly looked like a wolf pup at all. He blinked a couple of times, as if he was trying out his eyelids to see if they actually worked, and his expression was vague. "Abban?" His mother crouched down beside him and whispered, "You've had a bad fall, dear. But you're fine." There was an inflection that made Caila's last words more of a question than a statement. "I'll warm you up in no time." She began to lick him ferociously, and Mhairie and Dearlea rushed to help her. After a minute, his shivering lessened.

"Abban, can you talk to me?" Caila asked. "Say something." He looked at her, but there was still a vagueness in his green eyes. Mhairie stopped licking and crouched down directly in front of him.

"Abban. It's me — Mhairie. Your sister."

Still he said nothing. But the light in his eyes had grown brighter, and his shivering had stopped completely. And then he opened his mouth, and the words squeaked out. "You licked the sea right off of me."

"He spoke!" Caila said jubilantly, but she did not notice the wistfulness in Abban's voice.

He whispered, "I spoke, I spoke, but it was the tooth that gave the poke and then the water around me broke."

"What's he saying?" Mhairie asked.

"I don't know," Dearlea replied. "But he sounds a little . . . a little strange."

"Not at all!" Caila snapped. "My pup is fine. Perfectly fine!"

Dearlea brought Abban a lemming that he consumed with gusto. Then Edme gently approached him and asked if he was ready to go on. The little pup looked at her in the most curious way. His eyes grew larger and seemed to have taken on the watery greenness of the depths to which he had plunged.

"Are you all right? Do you think you're ready to travel again?" Edme repeated.

"Am I ready?" He paused as if to consider Edme's question further, and then replied in a rather singsongy voice, "Go forth we must or turn to dust."

Caila blinked at her son. "Say again, Abban?"

"Say again? Again I say. But heed it not be gainsay."

The creatures looked at one another, each wondering why Abban was speaking in this odd manner. Finally, Katria stepped forward.

"I think Abban is ready to go. Aren't you, Abban?" And this time the little wolf nodded solemnly and did not utter a single word.

Twilight was falling. Faolan glanced up at the sky, looking for any sign of Molgith, the first star in the star ladder that led to spirit trail, and finally to the constellation of the Cave of Souls. But things were slightly different or rearranged in this part of the world. The stars that had risen with such predictability in the Beyond, shifting in expected increments as the seasons changed, did not behave the same way here at all. Although he knew it was implausible, Faolan sometimes wondered if the terrible quakes that had convulsed the earth had shaken the very pillars of the sky, jiggled loose the familiar constellations they had known. Strangest of all, Beezar, the blind and staggering old wolf constellation that never appeared at this time of year, had followed the travelers west. It seemed ominous that this stumbling old wolf had been the only constellation to accompany them.

"Mind the pups and the cubs," Faolan barked. "Keep them close."

Caila picked up Abban in her mouth and began to carry him as one would a milking pup just out of the whelping den. Myrrglosch pressed in close to Edme. The bear cubs were much larger than the pups, but still the Whistler noticed how they crowded close between Airmead and Katria, the large, strong she-wolves of the once great MacNamara clan. And Banja, like Caila, picked up her pup, Maudie, in her mouth.

Maudie squirmed and protested, "Mum, I'm not a baby anymore!"

But Banja, her mouth firmly clamped on her pup's nape, merely snorted.

A snort could speak volumes, especially one coming from Banja, Edme thought. Who would have ever imagined that the cantankerous red wolf who had taken such delight in berating the new gnaw wolves at the Ring of Sacred Volcanoes would have been capable of the deep and tender love she had for her pup? It seemed to Edme that it was not simply a pup that had been born, but a whole new Banja as well.

The little brigade trudged on. Faolan looked back nervously every few steps to make sure they were safe. At the first sign of the wind strengthening, he barked the command *Vrychtong!* This was Old Wolf for "hunker down." The creatures wondered a bit as to why he was speaking in such an ancient dialect. It really was not a spoken language any longer and was rarely encountered except in the legal language of the complex codes and laws of the Beyond that ordered all aspects of the wolves' lives, and that had been gnawed into bones from times long past.

But for Edme, suddenly Old Wolf had a new resonance. *Or is it an old one?* she wondered. She felt again the deep pain in her hip. She gripped harder the bone she always carried. This, too — the pain in her hip and in her jaws — seemed to be echoes from a long ago past. What was it? She swung her head around to look at Faolan. Their eyes locked.

She senses it, he thought. *She teeters on the edges of my gyres. But how?* How could she ever know, Faolan wondered, that there were lives within him that were almost as old as time? He was, after all, not simply a silver wolf, a wolf of the Beyond, but a *gyre* wolf. The splayed paw had marked Faolan as a *malcadh*, but the swirling lines marked him as a *gyre* soul.

Before he was Faolan, he had lived as Eo, a grizzly bear. And before Eo, he had been Fionula, a Snowy Owl, and not a male but a female. However, his very first life, his very first soul, had been that of a wolf. And not just any wolf, but Fengo. Thus he had been named and thus thousands of years before, he had led a starving, ragtag band of wolves out of the Distant Blue and the land of the Long Cold to the east, and to the Beyond, a journey he was reversing now. He had become known as the Fengo, and the first chieftain of the Ring of Sacred Volcanoes. His name had become an honored title, and the title was inherited by scores of other Fengos through-out the centuries.

But the creatures he now led back to the Distant Blue knew none of this — except possibly for Edme. All this passed through Faolan's mind as their eyes remained locked. And yet they spoke not a word, for what would they say? What could they say? As she clenched the bone in her teeth, he could almost feel the pain in her hip. It was as if it were a shared pain, and he knew that there was within Edme something that was timeworn, time-tested, or perhaps time-lost. She had none of the markings of a *gyre* soul, but the way she walked now with an odd twist to her gait and that bone she carried were like distant whispers stirring inklings within him. The ancient bone, a femur, continued to tantalize him. He thought it was the loveliest of bones, with intricate gnaw marks that had faded until they were nearly indecipherable.

The bone had been revealed to him in the Cave Before Time, when a spike of moonlight had fallen on it through a crack in the ceiling. And it was at that same moment that Faolan had encountered his first *gyre* — Fengo. It had all happened at once, or so it seemed in retrospect. He had brought the bone with him, but Edme soon took charge of it. The carvings were in Old Wolf, and though she knew far less of Old Wolf than he did, she seemed to sense more about the bone than he could. It might have been his imagination, but he felt that when she carried it, her limp diminished somewhat. Now she broke their gaze. She turned and limped off, clutching the bone in her teeth, and with each step she took, the pain he had shared with her dimmed, faded as a star might fade in the light of dawn. He wanted it back. He wanted so desperately to take a share of her pain.

CHAPTER FOUR

DON'T BLAME THE BLUE

IT HAD BEEN A VERY LONG DAY starting with Abban's fall into the Frozen Sea. The ridges they'd crossed had been too numerous to count, and the animals now sank down under the overhanging lip of one that would afford excellent protection from the building wind. Clambering up to the top of the pressure ridge, Faolan and Edme took guard duty for the first watch of the night, digging their toes in deep to grip the ice against the gusts. Faolan tipped his head up. There again was Beezar the blind wolf clawing his way high into the sky. *Are you following us or leading us?* he wondered. He had never before noticed the two stars in Beezar's port hind leg that comprised the hock joint between the knee and the fetlock. Beneath the blind wolf, lined up with his stumbling forepaw, which was made of half a dozen stars,

Faolan could see scores of ridges rising and knew the next day would be as hard as the one they had just traveled.

The wind began to lessen until it was just a low ground whisper stirring ice crystals into slow sparkling dances around their paws, and the two wolves began to walk the top of the ridge, scanning for intruders. Caila had told them that she was sure Heep would follow and that his rout of outclanner wolves outnumbered their own brigade. The thought of so many savage wolves under the command of Heep was unsettling to Faolan. Heep was one of the most ruthless wolves on earth — malevolent, contemptible, and driven by the darkest instincts. He was a leader, but was he really leading his rout to anything other than certain death? Faolan was beginning to feel trapped, trapped between the threat behind them and the peril of the unknown ahead. What awaited them — a watery death if the bridge ended or this ice world warmed and simply melted away? As the night grew darker, the haze of the Distant Blue beyond the ridges seemed reproachful, perhaps even mocking. Edme passed by on her round and stopped.

"Don't blame the Blue," she said softly.

"What?"

"You know what I mean, Faolan." She nudged his

withers with her muzzle. "You're looking at all those ridges and the Distant Blue . . . and . . ." Her port forepaw shot out, and she slammed it down on a lemming that had just crept from an ice hole.

"Midnight snack?" she said.

"No, thank you. I've had quite enough for one day." Faolan looked at her as she tore the lemming apart and began to eat it. He could hear the tiny bones cracking with her first bite.

It was uncanny, he thought, how Edme always knew what he was thinking. It was as if she could crawl right inside his head.

"I'm not blaming the Blue, as you put it. If anything, it's the Ice Bridge. It looked so perfectly smooth when we first saw it. So glistening. I feel as if we've been deceived."

"But, Faolan, the agents of this deception, as you call it, are the same ones that cause mirages — which are a part of nature. An optical phenomenon. You know, we saw them all the time around the Ring. Remember when it was very cold and the volcanoes became active and the light of the flames would seem to bend? The sky above looked all funny and odd, as if it had come down to earth and taken on strange shapes that seemed so real. It was as if lakes suddenly formed around the Ring."

"So you're saying that this Ice Bridge was a mirage?"

"Not literally, for here we stand on it. But I am just saying the distortions of air and distance and light caused it to look very smooth and, well . . . spotless. Like a well-aged bone, bleached by the sun and polished by time."

"And not yet gnawed by wolves."

Edme laughed.

"Well, not gnaw wolves."

The Whistler and Airmead leaped onto the ridge for the second watch.

"Go off and get some sleep," Airmead said. "You both need it. It's been a hard day."

"There are more ridges, unfortunately, for tomorrow. As many as today if not more," Faolan said.

"We'll do it," the Whistler replied staunchly. "One paw in front of the other. We'll get there."

With such steadfast companions, Faolan knew that it was an indulgence for him to think about mirages or what he thought of as deceptions of nature. He retreated to a cavity at the base of the ridge overhung by a drapery of icicles. He made three tight circles, as was customary for wolves before they settled down. But seconds later, he rose and circled again. Sleep would be hard to come by, even if he had a soft caribou pelt beneath him instead of ice. He groaned when he thought how long it had been since he had slept on a caribou or elk pelt. Even as a gnaw wolf, the lowest-ranking wolf in the MacDuncan clan, they would often toss him a scrap of bare hide to sleep on. Now that would seem like a veritable luxury. It was all relative, he supposed. Would he ever sleep on something that made ice seem like sumptuous bedding material? He hoped not.

He looked out once more, and this time, he glimpsed the tail of Beezar. But an even more perplexing question was that of another constellation, the one they had glimpsed just before they had stepped onto the Ice Bridge at the end of the Crystal Plain. Had it been a dream when they had watched that burst of a dozen stars or more that had inexplicably sorted themselves into a configuration none of them had ever seen in the heavens before? The shape etched in stars was that of a container — not just any container, but a memory jug of the Sark of the Slough. They had found the Sark after the earthquake, dying in her cave on a bed of shards from the shattered memory pots, which had once contained her recollections of the many scents she had encountered and somehow committed to the clay jugs she fashioned in her kiln.

The Sark was a strange, irascible creature, hideous in

many ways to look at with her skittish eye and mangy pelt. She had been feared by many for no reason other than her oddness. They whispered she was a witch, because she had skills with fire that only owls were supposed to possess. Yet the Sark had been Faolan's staunchest ally and Gwynneth's oldest friend in the Beyond. Her loss was a terrible one, leaving both the wolf and the Masked Owl as shattered as the pots on which the Sark had died. How they had begged her to rally. As Faolan looked out through the fringe of icicles, he remembered her last words to him and to Gwynneth: *I am here with my pot shards, on a bed of fractured memories slowly coming back together. This is my heaven, my Cave of Souls.* She had looked at Gwynneth. *My Glaumora.* She had reached out with a shaking paw to touch Faolan's shoulder lightly, and then whispered, *And my Ursulana.*

But there was no use thinking about the Sark. She was dead. Her bones were moldering among the fragments of her memory pots. Faolan knew that it was not because of the Sark that he couldn't sleep, and it wasn't this bed of ice. It was the little ones, the pups and the cubs, Toby and Burney. Even though the bear cubs were many times bigger than the pups, they were still vulnerable. It was not always size but maturity that counted.

What he really had to do was focus on how to protect the little ones.

He heard Edme's familiar footsteps and could tell that her hind leg was bothering her. But that was a forbidden subject. She appeared behind the scrim of icicles that glistened fierce and sharp as fangs in the moonlight.

"You're up, I see."

"Well, so are you, Edme."

"Want to talk a bit?" She opened her single eye wider. The lovely green light that emanated from it seemed to dissolve the ice teeth and take the sting from the air. Her face appeared almost luminous.

"Of course I do. You always know when I need you, don't you?" Faolan got up and came out from beneath the ridge's overhang where he had been attempting to sleep. They had shared much in their years as Watch wolves, but he wanted so much more. Was he becoming a foolish wolf? Perhaps. But there was no time for foolishness. Fools could not carry the worries he did.

"How do you always seem to know?" He suddenly realized that this might be a dangerous question. "I mean" — he hesitated — "you always know when I want to talk."

"No, not really, but it's easy to see you're still worried about Abban."

"It's not just Abban. I'm worried about all the little ones. What happened today could happen again. Lupus knows how that pup ever bobbed back up to the surface, and thank Glaux that Gwynneth got to him!"

Edme realized how agitated Faolan really was. He was invoking two different animal spirits at the same time, Lupus and Glaux. Could "Urskadamus," his favorite bear curse, be far behind?

"Try to stay calm, Faolan," she counseled, but the words sounded weak even to her own ears.

"But it could happen tomorrow, Edme! Don't you see?" Faolan paused. He shut his eyes tight as he tried to envision that crucial painting in the Cave Before Time, which he had first glimpsed when he was hardly a yearling and seen many times since. It was a picture of a flowing line of wolves. He had not even known the word then but would soon learn the configuration was called a *byrrgis*, the seminal formation that wolves used for traveling and hunting. It was absolutely critical to their lives. It was what made wolves truly strategic hunters and was at the very core of wolf civilization. He opened his eyes now.

"Edme, the *byrrgis* is useless on this Ice Bridge." He felt something wither in him as he said these nearly

32

sacrilegious words, and indeed Edme looked at him for just a moment as if he were some kind of infidel. He could hardly believe what he was saying. But he knew that it was true.

Nevertheless it did not alter the fact that the *byrrgis* was as sacred to wolf culture as the Great Chain, the order that linked the wolves from the heavens to the land. The first link in that chain was Lupus, the spirit wolf, and was represented in the glittering constellation of the Great Wolf. The first carving lesson for every gnaw wolf in every clan was to incise this chain on a clean bone. By carving it on their gnaw bones, the chain over time became engraved in the very marrow of every wolf. No wolf knew the Great Chain better, experienced it more deeply, than the lowest-ranking wolves — the gnaw wolves, which Faolan, Edme, and the Whistler had all been. The *byrrgis* formation, in a sense, was an expression of that chain. In a *byrrgis*, wolves moved in a very pre-scribed order. And now Faolan was saying this order was useless, obsolete.

"What are you suggesting?" Edme asked.

He looked up into the sky, scanning it for a familiar star formation and wondering if that strange one, the starry configuration of the Sark's memory jug, would ever appear again. Had it been a figment of his imagination? But they had all seen it. Still, this sky felt foreign to him.

"Do you remember that last night, before we started on the Ice Bridge, when we saw that constellation that looked exactly like one of the Sark's memory jugs?"

"Yes, but what does that have to do with the *byrrgis* on the bridge?"

"Everything has changed since we started on the Ice Bridge, even the skies! There are new constellations. Ones we've never seen. It makes me think that we must invent new ways of doing things."

"Like what?" Edme narrowed her single eye until it was just a thin slit of green light.

"A new formation, a practical formation for the Ice Bridge. Instead of a long line, like the *byrrgis*, we need a configuration that is designed specifically to protect the small creatures, the youngest and most vulnerable."

"What would it look like?"

"Odd," Faolan replied, and began to drag one of his claws across the ice. When he finished, there was a slightly askew square inscribed on the ice. "You see, Edme, the littlest ones — Maudie, Myrr, Abban, Toby, and Burney — would be in the middle. Toby and Burney would be on the outer flanks of the middle."

"Sort of like defensive guards in a *byrrgis?*"

"Yes, a cross between a defensive guard and a wide rounder, but we are not in a line, as you can see. The bear cubs are the biggest of all the young animals in the center of this formation. But you get the idea. We shall basically be moving across this bridge like . . . like . . ."

"Like a fortress against the wind," Edme replied.

"Yes," Faolan said, looking out to sea. "Look! Look out there!"

"What is it?" Edme squinted with her one eye.

"It looks like another crack opening, like the one Abban fell into. 'Leads,' that was what Gwynneth said they called these cracks in the northern kingdoms. They are like passageways."

"Passageways exactly! Look! Look what's passing through!"

"Great Lupus, what are those things?"

Was it some sort of *byrrgis*, a *byrrgis* through the sea? For there was a procession of swimming creatures — were they fish? A softly explosive sound followed by a plume of spray announced their presence, then the water parted, revealing their long dappled gray-and-black backs that glimmered in the moonlight. They were immense, larger than any fish Faolan or Edme had ever seen. The two wolves were startled to notice that these sea creatures breathed air. It was all very odd. The winds had stilled, the ice had parted, and beneath the utter silence of the dome of the night, the great sea beasts came. But what were they? They were wrapped in the profound mysteries of the sea, and yet they breathed the air of the earth.

Gwynneth swooped down and landed beside Faolan and Edme.

"Do you see what's coming?" The Masked Owl twisted her head almost completely around and then flipped it upside down for a better look at the creatures making their way through the lead in the ice.

"We see them," Edme replied, "but we don't know what they are."

"Narwhales," Gwynneth answered.

"Narwhales?" Faolan asked. "I've heard of whales, but narwhales?"

"They're rare, even in the northern kingdoms. When I went there with my father years and years ago, we only spotted one the whole summer. But there are at least thirty in this pod."

"But what are those . . . those . . ." Edme squinted harder, trying to bring into focus the strange long objects that stuck out of the water.

"Spears?" Gwynneth asked.

"Yes, exactly," Faolan said. "It looks like something you might have smithed in your forge. Is it a weapon?"

"A natural weapon, I suppose. It's actually a very long tooth. Narwhales feed on the flat fish that live beneath the ice, and maybe they can skewer them right up with that long tooth."

"But most creatures have teeth in their mouths, not stuck on the end of their faces!"

"It just appears to be on the face. But it is actually in the whale's mouth. It grows out of its upper jaw. Port side," Gwynneth explained. "They can dive very deep, deeper than any other sea creature. They swim very deep, except when they come up to blow, like now. But they can be down on the bottom for a very long time."

"How curious," Edme said.

"You know something even more curious?"

"What?"

"I think that when little Abban fell into the sea . . ." Gwynneth hesitated. "I actually think he saw these creatures."

"What?" Faolan and Edme both said at once.

"That's impossible!" Edme said. "He would have had to have gone all the way to the bottom. You just said they swim deep . . . how . . . how . . ." She was stammering.

"Abban saw them, I'm sure. When he broke back

through the surface and I grabbed him, he was babbling about a strange water beast with a sword or tusk or something. It seemed utter nonsense at the time."

Faolan also recalled Abban whispering something about a tooth just after he resurfaced. He looked out on the narwhales plying their way through the channels. "He could have been speared by that tusk and killed," Faolan whispered.

"No, Faolan." Gwynneth shook her head. "Quite the reverse. I think the narwhales saved him."

"You saved him, Gwynneth!" Edme protested.

"But don't you see? They — the narwhales — brought him to the surface. Very gently so as not to pierce him with their long tooth."

"It's unimaginable," Edme said softly.

Gwynneth nodded somberly. "Abban has been to places we've never even dreamed of, and what he saw down there is beyond anything."

They watched in silence as the narwhales, scores of them, threaded their way through the channel in the ice. Their tusks waved eerily in the rising mist like swords in the fog of some mystical war.

CHAPTER FIVE

THE FORTRESS

THE NEW *BYRRGIS* WAS A FORtress, but it was awkward. Much more awkward for the wolves than the bears, Gwynneth thought as she looked down at the unusual shape moving beneath her. She always enjoyed flying above a *byrrgis*. There was a grace to the sinuous line of wolves, each fleet animal stretching to its fullest length as they sped across the landscape. It had always stirred her gizzard.

Gwynneth knew the wolves' individual running styles. By its legs or the posture of its tail, she could tease a single wolf from the strand of motion. Once, in her forge, she had taken hammer and tongs to metal and made a long tapering piece that perfectly captured the undulations of a *byrrgis*. How many magpies had hounded her to barter that ribbon of bright metal? But she never would. She hung it in the single tree by her forge and would watch it dance in the wind, its spangles of light splashing across the hard ground of the Beyond. It was gone now, buried in the debris of the earthquake. She had searched for it but finally given up. It was just one of the many things she left behind, along with her hammers, tongs, and anvils, the tools of her trade.

So much had been left behind. So little taken along and now even the *byrrgis* formation was gone. What was this new lumpy thing that moved across the bridge with all the delicacy of a herd of musk ox? She understood Faolan's reasoning — it was logical and made sense, but it certainly was not beautiful. She wondered if there would be a place for beauty in the new world they were traveling toward. This Distant Blue. Would there be a place for her? A Rogue smith without her tools. A Rogue smith whose vision was dimming.

Everyday things seemed to grow fainter for Gwynneth. At first, she thought it was temporary; perhaps the harsh winds had blown something in her eyes. But no matter how often she swiped them with the thin, transparent membrane that allowed owls to clear their eyes, her vision still seem clouded. They had been very careful not to cross the Crystal Plain in the full light of day, but perhaps she had flown out too early on some days to scout and had burned her pecten, the delicate folded tissue behind her lens. She knew an old Snowy who had scarred her pecten somehow. Watching her take off and land was pathetic, a terrible thing to witness, for she could not orient herself between land and sky. The Snowy finally died of a broken neck when she crash-landed. A horrific crash. Every one of those fourteen neck bones that allow an owl to turn its head almost completely around was broken.

Gwynneth looked down and saw the ungainly lump of wolves drawing to a halt under the pressure ridge below her. The wind had quickened. To scale the ridge even in this fortress formation was risky. She angled her wings and went into a steep banking turn.

"We're camping here for the night?" Gwynneth asked the creatures huddled under the narrow overhang of the glacier.

"No, we're just stopping temporarily. We'll wait for a break in the wind," Edme replied.

"A break?" Gwynneth turned to Faolan just as there was an ominous creak in the pressure ridge. "This is what might break," Gwynneth said, flipping her head almost upside down to gesture toward the overhang.

"I know," Faolan replied. "This is not a good place to linger." He felt another kind of pressure ridge forming in his own marrow. At this moment, the travelers were trapped between the wind and the threat of breaking ice. But if they tried to scale the ridge, they could not maintain the fortress formation and risked one of the young ones being scraped off by the howling wind. But what if they took each of the young ones singly? An adult on each side with a pup pressed between them? It might work, and Toby and Burney were not so little. They could surely get over the top without too much trouble. It was worth a try.

"Here's what we are going to do." Faolan gathered the brigade around him and began to explain.

"Me first!" Myrr cried.

Abban blinked, remained silent for a moment, then spoke, "Better a fool fast than a fool last."

The Whistler cocked his head. "Huh?"

Caila drew her pup close. "It's nothing." Her eyes darted around nervously to the others "He's . . . he's still not quite himself yet. But he'll be perfect, back to his old self soon. Just a bit of a shock." She snapped her head around and settled her eyes on Airmead, the pure white wolf who had once been an Obea for the MacHeath clan, charged with the grim task of taking *malcadhs* from their mothers. Caila shoved her ears forward and assumed a confrontational posture. "You try falling into the sea, Airmead. You might come back babbling a bit and not sounding quite yourself."

Airmead shrank back and tension laced the air, but then Abban piped up. "Self, mum? Self? How many selves does one pup need? A self for here. A self for there, and one that goes everywhere!"

There was a nervous silence. Faolan growled as if to clear his throat.

"Well, let's begin. Myrr, you'll be first. I'll be on your port flank, and Edme will be on your starboard flank."

"Ready?" Edme asked.

"Oh, yes," the little pup replied.

"You're going to have to dig in your front toe claws to pull and use the back ones to push and we'll try to help you all we can," Edme said.

"I have very strong toe claws," Myrr said.

And so they started. Faolan and Edme pressed in on either side of Myrr. They advanced slowly up the slope of the ridge. Squashed between them, Myrr could feel both their hearts beating. *Beating for me*, he thought, and wistfully recalled the sound of his own mother's heartbeat when he had nursed as a very young pup. But she was gone and he was here, sheltered by two wolves with whom he did not share one drop of blood but who cared for him as if he were their own. He hoped he would never do anything that would make them turn their backs on him as his mum and da had. He knew it was not his fault his parents had left. Edme had drummed that into him. She became quite upset when Myrr would sometimes ask what it was about him that made them leave. Edme always replied almost crossly, "It wasn't you, Myrrglosch. It was them! They were sick, dear. Now let's hear no more about it."

He treasured the sound and the pulse of Edme's and Faolan's hearts. He had heard of rocks that were thought to be very precious. They were called jewels and they were meant to be lustrous and dazzling to the eye. Some creatures bartered their souls for them, but right now, little Myrr felt that he possessed something more valuable than the brightest jewel — the sound of these two hearts beating close to his own.

They were nearing the top of the ridge when a huge blast struck like an anvil. Would the fortress against the wind hold? Myrr felt himself begin to slip. He closed his eyes tight and held his breath. Faolan's and Edme's beating hearts pounded through him. *I might die . . . I might die . . . but I am loved.* And the world turned as bright as the most brilliant diamond.

Bone in my teeth, claw in pup's withers. That was the only thought in Edme's head. *If I can hold the withers and clench the bone, we shall be all right.* They were tumbling into what seemed a free fall. She was not sure which side of the ridge they were on — the slope they had tried to climb or the far side. She felt no traction under her paws. She sensed Faolan was somehow holding on to Myrr, as she was. But were they flying?

Then they stopped, but the impact was not hard at all. They had slid onto a mound of snow, the three of them so entangled it was difficult to sort out whose limbs were whose.

"What luck! A snowbank!" Faolan exclaimed as he extricated his back legs from Edme's forelegs. They could both feel Myrr squirming beneath them. The pup staggered to his feet.

"Snow? But there's only been ice for days," Myrr said.

"It came from down there," Edme said, nodding toward the edge of the Frozen Sea. "We're in some sort of eddy."

"An eddy with lemmings," Faolan said, for dozens of the furry rodents began squirming out of the snow.

They quickly dispatched enough of the rodents that there would be sufficient meat for all of them. As Myrr finished tearing the legs off the one he was eating, he looked up, his muzzle covered with blood, and asked, "What's an eddy?"

"It's like a whirlpool," Faolan replied, still chewing on one of the plumper lemmings. "The wind gets caught going round and round, opposite to the main current, and it picks up the snow that blankets the sea ice and blows it here where it got caught. See how the ridge curves on this side? It makes a cup to catch the wind and the snow. And so we're safe!"

"You're safe!" Gwynneth hooted from above, and then tilted her wings as if coming in for a landing.

"She's flying kind of funny," Myrr said.

"No. Not really," Faolan replied. "She's crabbing."

"Crabbing?"

"It's a way owls have of flying against the wind. They angle toward it, rather than meeting it head-on."

Edme looked up. She'd seen more than one owl crab in her day, but there was something peculiar about the way Gwynneth was flying and it was not just the angle. She seemed hesitant, as if she could not line up her approach glide for a landing.

"What's she doing up there?" Faolan asked. "I thought she was coming in to land."

"Me, too," Edme said.

Faolan watched as Gwynneth angled her wings more steeply and ruddered her tail. She swooped down, her legs and talons extended into the landing positions, but suddenly she retracted them and flapped her wings to power straight up.

"*Tine smyorfin!*" Faolan exploded with the Old Wolf oath, a swear of the marrow. "What in the name of Ursus is she doing?"

"Here she comes again," Edme said.

"She's crashing!" Myrr screeched.

There was a flurry of feathers. Some downy ones were caught in the breeze and swirled overhead as Gwynneth plowed into the snowbank.

Gwynneth's head popped up from the snow, and she screeched, "Crashing! Absolutely not! I did not crash!" It was an angry, shrill sound unique to members of the Barn

Owl family and made when they were perturbed or alarmed. She shook off the snow covering her wings, then swung her head toward the wolf pup. Her eyes narrowed until they were just black slits, and her beak trembled as if she were trying to get a grip on her next words. "For your information, that was an excellent landing given the conditions. Those were shredder winds. If you haven't heard the term or are not familiar with such winds, I suggest that you visit the Canyonlands in the Hoolian empire. I can give you the coordinates if you care! There is a region in the Canyonlands so renowned for its savage winds it is known simply as the Shredders. I flew them when I was not much more than a hatchling."

Gwynneth let out a hideous screech again, and Faolan could see she was beyond indignation. Faolan was shocked by her vitriol.

"Yes, yes, I've heard of the Shredders," he lied. He was desperate to soothe the angry Masked Owl. "And I think we encountered much the same thing when we reached the summit of this ridge. We all came tumbling down."

Gwynneth sniffed. "I did not tumble! What I executed is technically known as a three-point landing. Both talons and a tail."

"Yeah, your tail looks kind of bashed up," Myrr said.

Oh, great Lupus, why did he have to say that? Edme was ready to pounce on Myrr.

"If you have problems with my tail —" Gwynneth took a step toward the pup and almost snarled now.

"No one has problems with your tail!" Edme said quickly, and glared at Myrr. "Your tail is fine."

Gwynneth flipped her head upside down and twisted it all the way around to examine her rear plummage. "I might have lost a feather or two." She was standing on three feathers, but Faolan knew better than to mention it. "They're just coverts. My tail is fully functional. Perfectly serviceable."

"I'm sure it is," Faolan said. "Now all of you stay here. I'm going to scramble back over to the other side and give the rest some suggestions on how to negotiate this ridge and the shredder winds on top."

"I could fly over myself and tell them quicker," Gwynneth offered.

"It's not necessary for you to fly back over the ridge. And you know yours is the view from the sky and we of course have four paws on the ground. So it's a bit different."

"I see," Gwynneth said, suddenly docile. "I thought I

could tell them about the lemmings we have waiting for them. They seem a bit hungry."

"I doubt that the thought of more lemmings would be a thrill, seeing as that is all we've eaten for days," Edme said. "Well, at least until the last couple of days, because we haven't come across many recently. A little diversity to our diet would do wonders for the spirits. There's really no need for you to fly back over to announce lemmings."

Gwynneth had felt her gizzard flinch when Faolan had said *yours is the view from the sky*. The problem was that in this terrible landscape, she could hardly tell the sky from the ground. Everything was white — the Ice Bridge, the Frozen Sea from which it rose. White, just white. And though they drew closer every day, the Distant Blue seemed to fade for her until it was just a blur on the horizon.

CHAPTER SIX

A Pup Sleepwalks

ALL OF THEM, ALL FIFTEEN CREA-
tures, safely made it to the top of the ridge and slid down
the far side. Neither pup nor cub was scraped off by the
ferocious winds. Faolan had decided that they would
camp there for the night, burrowing into the soft snow
that had been blown up by the eddies swirling on the
Frozen Sea. The animals were exhausted, and the drift of
snow that had kept building throughout the day offered
their first soft bed since they had begun their journey
on the Ice Bridge. In the future, they would learn where
to look for these drifts on the bridge. They discovered
that it was easy to hollow them out, and they were so
comfortable that the animals began to call them "snugs,"
or "snow snugs." And thus a new word came into their
language as they made their way across the Ice Bridge to
the Distant Blue.

Mhairie and Dearlea were on watch. They did not patrol the ridge, as it was too dangerous with the sudden gusts of wind and it was unimaginable that Heep or any other creature could steal up and over it while the travelers slept. But they had realized quickly that the Frozen Sea itself could serve as a way around this particular ridge if it had not been cracked by too many leads. So they kept a sharp lookout over the sea.

"You know," said Dearlea, "although we're worried about a rout sneaking up on us by coming over the Frozen Sea, we should think about it as a way for ourselves to travel."

"Out there? You mean on the ice?" Mhairie asked, looking toward the vast icescape that stretched around them endlessly. The ice was not flat, as river ice was in the Beyond, but had been frozen into rhythmic undulations that mimicked the swells of a sea. It was as if a single moment in the coldest depths of winter had been captured, as if a movement had been arrested and the sea ice was sculpted into soft, billowing waves. "Yes. If we could be certain that there were not cracks in the ice, it would be possible to go out there. It looks a bit easier. There are no ridges to climb over."

"But the Ice Bridge also looked flat when we first saw it," Mhairie replied.

"That's true, but we're closer to the Frozen Sea than we were when we first glimpsed the Ice Bridge." Dearlea paused a moment. "Odd, isn't it, how when we first started out we called the sea the western sea but now we always call it the Frozen Sea."

Mhairie reflected a minute. "Gwynneth said that in the Hoolian empire, before the owls crossed the Sea of Vastness and discovered the Sixth Kingdom, they called that ocean the Unnamed Sea, and there was a place in the northern kingdoms that has been called the Nameless Region for centuries."

"Interesting, very intriguing," Dearlea said pensively. Mhairie was quiet. She recognized from her sister's tone that she was thinking deeply. "It's as if," Dearlea continued, "before we know, before we experience something, we can't really name it. To name it is to know it."

"I wonder what we'll name the Distant Blue when we get to it," Mhairie asked in a musing voice.

Dearlea swung her head about, her eyes bright and eager. "Now, that's an excellent question! What will we name the Distant Blue when we finally get there?" She blinked, and a sudden shadow seemed to flit through the luminous green of her eyes.

"What's wrong?" Mhairie asked.

"Oh, dear."

"What is it?" Mhairie asked again, and then turned in the direction her sister was looking. She inhaled sharply. Their little brother, Abban, was walking below them, stiff legged.

The pup's eyes were wide open, but there was an enormous vacancy in them.

"He must be sleepwalking. But . . . but . . . it's like he's gone *by-lang*."

In the language of wolves, *by-lang* literally meant "deeply away." Often, pregnant female wolves, particularly if they sensed they might be giving birth to a *malcadh*, went *by-lang*. Troubled wolves who wandered off were said to go *by-lang*. But Abban appeared to be sleepwalking and not running as a *by-lang* wolf would.

They scrambled down to their brother. "What should we do?" Mhairie whispered.

"I'm not sure. But I think it can be dangerous to wake a wolf when it is sleepwalking. Remember the tale that Alastrine told." Dearlea had been a student of the old *skreeleen* of the MacDuncan clan and was due to inherit her title until the earthquake came and killed the few wolves who hadn't died in the famine. There were no clans left, and no one left to *skree* for, no one to listen to the old stories.

"You mean the tale of the mother who had become separated from her pup and began to wander in her sleep?" Mhairie asked.

"Exactly, and her mate came up to her in the night and tried to wake her and she mistook him for a cougar she had been dreaming about, whom she suspected of killing her pup. So when her mate woke her, she struck at him and raked out his eyes."

"Oh, Lupus!" Mhairie's voice was tight. Her hackles bristled as their brother Abban closed the distance between them. He was still much smaller than they were, but if he were startled, there was no telling what he might do.

"I think we should stand here very still. Not move one bit," Dearlea whispered.

The pup walked by them. His body was there, but it was as if a thief had come in the night and stolen his soul. He looked glazed, untenanted. Abban walked the palsied gait of an old and feeble wolf, and though his green eyes appeared to register nothing, he seemed in some way wistful for something unrecoverable, something that haunted him.

Lemmings they complain of.
Lemmings here. Lemmings there.

Lemmings crawling everywhere.
But the riches of the deep
Where puffins find a special treat.
One by one they line them up,
then take them in a single gulp.

Faolan appeared and flicked his ears to signal that no noise must be made. The sisters realized that he had been following the pup on his sleepwalking expedition and must have guided him away from the edge of the bridge, where he could have fallen yet again into the Frozen Sea. He was herding Abban gently, like a mother caribou might herd her calf away from danger to safety. In this case, Faolan was guiding Abban back to the snow snug where Caila was sleeping soundly. Mercifully, Caila did not know her son had taken this nighttime wander. Mhairie and Dearlea watched the two wolves disappear around the bend in the ridge to where Caila slept.

Soon Faolan was back, alone. "Don't breathe a word of what you saw to anyone, especially not to Caila. She is practially out of her mind with worry about Abban. This will make her worse." The sisters both nodded. "He is a deeply disturbed little pup," Faolan continued.

"Is that why she growled at Airmead?" Dearlea asked.

"Was she fearful he was becoming like . . . like a *malcadh* with a twisted brain and Airmead would take him away?"

"Possibly. But Airmead would never do anything like that. Never! She's finished being an Obea."

"But . . . but . . ." Mhairie stammered. "Is . . . is . . . is he *cag mag*?" Mhairie asked.

Faolan's tail drooped. He seemed profoundly weary, depleted. "I'm not sure if I would call it *cag mag*. It's very different."

"How would you describe it?" Edme asked. She'd just appeared for her watch and had caught a glimpse of Faolan as he had guided Abban back to his mother.

"Perhaps he is out of his mind. But it is as if he has traveled to someplace else."

"This sleepwalking. It seems as if he was wrapped in some sort of delusion."

"But you see, that's just the point. I don't think it was a delusion. Abban has seen something none of us has ever seen. He's been to the bottom of the ocean!"

A flicker in the sky caught Faolan's attention, and he tipped his head up. "Look at that constellation, Edme. Have you ever seen one like it?"

"Not in the Beyond, never. But as you said, everything seems new here."

"How would you describe it?"

"I don't know. It's kind of fish-shaped, I guess. And it has a kind of long . . ." She turned toward Faolan and opened her eye very wide. "A long spear sticking up. A narwhale?"

Mhairie and Dearlea tipped their heads up as well, then turned and walked away toward their snug, leaving Faolan and Edme to their stargazing.

"That's it exactly!" Edme continued. "It's like the ones we saw the other evening when the lead opened up in the Frozen Sea and the procession of narwhales came through."

Faolan turned and looked out at the wind-whipped expanse of the Frozen Sea. Edme cocked her head and studied him. She had seen this posture, this angle of his head, this expression in his eyes so many times before. She knew better than to interrupt his thoughts. He would speak when he was ready.

Clouds streaked across the moon, quenching the light that silvered the ice. The wind stretched the clouds out until in her mind they took on the lean, fleet shapes of wolves — wolves in a *byrrgis* racing through the night at press-paw speed. And behind them, the new constellation of the Narwhale glimmered.

"Edme," Faolan said, turning to her. "What would you say if we went out there?" He tipped his head slightly to indicate where he had been looking.

She was startled. "Out there? You mean on the Frozen Sea?"

"Yes. It's something that Dearlea mentioned to me. It might be easier. Fewer pressure ridges."

Edme clamped her single eye shut. She could think of so many reasons why this was a terrible idea. But she had to stay calm.

Faolan regarded her. He knew exactly what she was trying to do. Whenever she clamped that lone eye shut, it meant that Edme was wrestling with her patience. And Edme was normally a very patient she-wolf.

"Faolan, there aren't as many ridges out there. But there are cracks, leads that we could fall into. The dangers are immense! What if we were on a piece of ice that broke? We would be instantly marooned on an iceberg. And if not that, suppose we get lost out there? Suppose we can't find our way back to the Ice Bridge? Then what? We would be aimlessly wandering forever." Edme's posture was not that of a frightened wolf, but a determined wolf. Her tail stuck straight out, her ears were shoved forward, and her single eye glared green. But beneath the harshness of the glare, something else spar-kled from her like the light from an ancient star.

"We could navigate by the stars," Faolan replied. "There is the Narwhale — look at it. His spear points west, to the Distant Blue, and Beezar, too, burns brightly. And there is Gwynneth. Owls know celestial navigation."

Edme felt a quiver pass through her marrow. She knew that Gwynneth was Faolan's oldest friend, his first friend in the Beyond. When he had made his way back from the Outermost after a fruitless search for his second Milk Giver, the grizzly bear Thunderheart, only to dis-cover that she was dead, it was Gwynneth who had found him howling his grief into the night. She had taken him to her forge, comforted him as best she could, and then told him gently that the time had come for him to seek out his clan. They had been fast friends ever since.

Was Faolan ready to admit what Edme was already sure of? That his oldest friend, Gwynneth, was going blind. He had seen her crash-landing in the snowdrift. But he had been quite short with Edme when she had started to question him about Gwynneth. Indeed, he had actually snapped at her, which he had almost never done before. *What do you mean she couldn't see us?* he'd said. *That's ridiculous! She saw us. It was the wind. I've heard about those Shredders. Those were the exact same conditions.*

Edme realized that this was not the time to bring up Gwynneth's eyesight. She would put it to rest and try a different tactic. "Look, we might be able to navigate by the stars with Gwynneth's help, yes. But those leads can open up quickly. We've seen it happen now at least twice. You hear a crack, and before you know it, you see a stretch of water."

"That's just it, Edme." He stepped closer to her and drew his muzzle to within inches of her own.

"What's just it, Faolan?"

"Abban. I spent the better part of this night following that poor pup about. As I said, I don't believe he is *cag mag* or out of his mind. It's more accurate to say that he's in another mind."

"What mind would that be?"

"The sea's."

Edme blinked with incomprehension. She was not following Faolan's thinking at all.

"Edme," Faolan continued, "I've been watching him carefully, ever since he fell in. You're right. Those leads open quickly with very little warning. But each time it happened, I saw Abban's hackles bristle up and his ears

61

flicker right before. He knows before we do, before any-body does, except the creatures in the deepest part of the sea." Faolan paused. "And he knows other things as well."

"What other things?"

"You heard when Gwynneth said it was the nar-whales that saved him?"

"Yes."

"Well, while he was sleepwalking, he kept talking about this one creature. Old Tooth he called him. It had to be a narwhale. We think he's a fool, but he's not. We think he talks nonsense, but it's just another kind of sense."

"What did he say about this narwhale?"

"Just before I got him back to Caila, he began again in that peculiar voice of his. It's not quite a howl but like a strange music — watery music. He said, *Old Tooth will warn, before it's born, the cracks that break, the ice like cakes* —" Faolan stopped abruptly.

"What else?" Edme asked.

The green in Faolan's eyes deepened. "Abban said, *The fool goes down. Comes back a clown, but from won-drous depths Old Tooth does sound.* Can't you see, Edme, that between the narwhale in the sky and the one who swims in the deep we might find our way safely across the ice to the Distant Blue?"

"Faolan . . . Faolan . . ." She was at a loss for how to respond. Faolan was her dearest friend. They had gone together into the Gaddergnaw Games as gnaw wolves and come out as wolves of the Watch. And beyond that, they seemed to share some sort of mystical bond that neither one of them quite understood. No matter what, she had always trusted Faolan and he had trusted her. Their trust was like a living thing — a bone flowing and quick with marrow. But Edme was now completely dumbfounded. A rush of warm emotions seemed to be flooding through her, and she didn't quite understand them. They were new and unexpected.

"I know, it's weird."

Weird. It is beyond weird, Edme thought.

"So what do you think?" Faolan asked.

Edme squared her shoulders. "Think? I think it's dangerous." She hesitated.

"But not *cag mag?*"

What a question, she thought. *We'd be relying on a wolf pup who, if not* cag mag, *was awfully close to it.* Edme inhaled deeply.

"Are you asking me who's more *cag mag* — you or Abban?" Edme asked. "I'm not sure if I can answer that."

63

Faolan wilted before her eyes. His tail drooped. He sank into an almost submissive posture. He suddenly seemed more pathetic than any gnaw wolf she had ever encountered. Edme could not abide this; she couldn't stand to see him like this.

Suddenly, Airmead and Katria both appeared. Their hackles were raised. An unexpected blast of moonlight bleached the ground and printed an immense winged shadow against the whiteness of the Ice Bridge.

CHAPTER SEVEN

EAGLES

THEY CAME FROM THE EAST. THERE was frost on their tail feathers and patches of ice on their wings. Their white heads blazed bright in the moonlight. Eagles were not at all like owls — they were not silent fly-ers. In their wake, they left contrails of ice crystals and whirlpools of snowflakes aroused by their powerful wings, as if they carried their own weather with them. When they alighted, folding their great wings, there was a sud-den brace of buffeting gusts. Edme noted with awe that the span of their wings was twice the length of a wolf from the tip of its tail to the tip of its nose.

"They're coming! The wind has shifted. It's strong behind them. They're closing the distance," shrilled the larger of the eagles.

Out of the corner of her eye, Edme caught another blur of feathers. It was Gwynneth landing.

Eagles had been rare in the Beyond. And they spoke with a Hoolian burr that was hard for Faolan and Edme to understand. But why had they come here to them, these huge, majestic birds? The creatures of the brigade were almost too astonished to speak. Finally, Faolan found his tongue.

"What? What are you saying?" Faolan had taken a step closer. "Who's coming?"

"The yellow wolf," replied the smaller eagle.

"Heep!" Gwynneth staggered to her feet after her bumpy landing. She looked utterly exhausted. Faolan and Edme exchanged glances. Had Gwynneth flown out and seen Heep, then found these eagles?

The wind stopped, and a pocket of silence enveloped them. But if one listened carefully, the brush of snow-flakes could be heard against the feathers of these immense birds.

Gwynneth continued, "I went out tonight to scout easterly from this ridge. I found Eelon and Zanouche." She nodded toward the eagles. "Friends of mine from Silverveil."

"And you say Heep is on our trail?" Edme asked. She seemed almost afraid to address the eagles directly. Although the owls of the Hoolian world had a long history with eagles, there had rarely been any exchanges between wolves and eagles in the Beyond except for the most tragic sort. Eagles were predators and had been known to pick off *malcadh* pups when they had been abandoned on *tummfraws*. This was natural and as it should be according to the wolf codes. However, these two eagles were standing before a wolf brigade that had three *malcadhs* — Faolan, Edme, and the Whistler. It was only by the grace of Lupus that they had not become fodder for these monarchs of the sky. It was an unnerving situation, to say the least. But the eagles were here to warn them of another danger — Heep!

"Yes. We've been shadowing them for a few days," Zanouche replied. "They are not as organized as you. Heep is a poor leader, but he inspires with false promises. The way has been hard for them, but the wind has now shifted. It's behind them, and they are making good progress. Some of the ridges that you have encountered have been scraped down by this new wind."

Eelon interrupted, "They are bad wolves. We know. When the famine struck, we went far beyond our home nest in Ambala to hunt. We saw these wolves and their routs. You do not need them in this new place you are going."

"Not at all!" Zanouche nodded her head. "Savages all of them."

"And you?" Faolan asked tentatively. "You came from Ambala?"

"What was Ambala is gone," Zanouche said. "The immense nest of our ancestors has fallen. It had been there hundreds of years. There is nothing to go back for. The few owls and eagles left decided to cross the Sea of Vastness to the Sixth Kingdom." She paused, then sniffed. "To each her own, I suppose."

"We decided to fly west," Eelon said. "Even though the wind was against us. But it finally changed."

"This new wind has not had the grace to reach us yet," the Whistler said, coming by on his watch.

Faolan cut in, "Tell me, what do you think of our leaving the bridge and striking out across the Frozen Sea?"

Eelon and Zanouche exchanged glances.

"It seems solid," Eelon began. "But one can never tell when a lead might open."

"Airmead and Katria might be all right in the water," Gwynneth said. "All the MacNamara wolves are good swimmers. They live near the Bittersea. It's been part of their training forever."

"But it hasn't really been part of ours," Edme said.

"Except for swimming after fish in the river. That's not quite the same thing."

"True," Eelon said. "But if the ice cracks, there is usually a period before a lead really begins to open up and you'd have time to make it back to the bridge." He looked at Gwynneth. "You have a good navigator here. Owls are known for that. Your aunt, the Rogue smith of Silverveil, was excellent."

"Y-y-yes. That she was. But, uh, the stars are different here. It . . . it can be quite disorienting."

"Gwynneth, I can help," Faolan said.

"How, Faolan? I don't understand."

"I have been studying these new star pictures." Faolan stepped up very close to Gwynneth's beak and peered into her black eyes. "Come with me to the edge of the bridge. The wind is down. I want you to look with me. See with me."

He knows, Edme thought. *He knows she is going blind. He has known. But he will not hurt her by admitting it. Was there ever a wolf so fierce and yet so tender?* Edme felt her heart swell.

The wolf and the owl stood close to each other on the very edge of the Ice Bridge. Faolan stooped low so he was level with Gwynneth's starboard ear slit. "Look to the east, Gwynneth. Just above the horizon." He was whispering.

"Yes." Her voice was slightly tremulous. "What is it you want me to see? There is a constellation that has a fluked tail, right?" She squinted. "Yes indeed, like that of a fish." The tremolo in her voice grew fainter.

"And a sort of bulbous head."

"Juglike almost, but not like any jug the Sark would make."

"Yes, juglike. Precisely, Gwynneth." He lifted a paw and tenderly patted her shoulder. "And now what do you see on the end of that juglike head?"

"It could be a scimitar like one my father once forged for the War of the Ember." Then she gasped. "Oh, Glaux in Glaumora! I see it now. It's the tusk of a narwhale!"

"Yes, and the scimitar points west. And the flukes of the tail point toward where we now stand on the Ice Bridge."

"Faolan." Gwynneth turned to her friend. "We'll never get lost if you keep the head to starboard and the tail, the port fluke of the tail, behind you. The bridge is perhaps two points off the port fluke."

"I don't understand points and all these . . . these . . ." Faolan stammered.

"The yonder?" Gwynneth asked softly.

"Yonder?" Faolan said.

"It's an old nestmaid-snake term for the sky. I told you that all the nestmaids at the Great Ga'Hoole Tree were blind. But they had an uncanny ability to perceive things they could not see, like the sky. Their sensibilities were very refined. They were very intuitive and could pick up on things missed by ordinary creatures, creatures who could see. I have thought about them a great deal recently." She sighed. "There was one very distinguished old nestmaid snake, Mrs. Plithiver was her name. She actually flew with Soren on occasion."

"King Soren?"

"Yes, but it began long before he was a king, when he was just a youngster. It was said that she once commented that the sky does not exist merely in the wings of birds, an impulse in their feathers and blood and bone, but that sky becomes the yonder for all creatures. It is your yonder, Faolan. I can tell. You know the stars, Faolan, even if these are different ones. You know how to navigate, even if you're a wolf. By Glaux, you're a star wolf if I have ever seen one."

Faolan blinked. Gwynneth was right, of course the yonder was his and always had been. But she didn't know just how right she was. She had no suspicion, no inkling of his previous life as a Snowy Owl who had wandered all of the Hoolian kingdoms, both those of the north and the south. Gadfeathers were the most restless of owls and ranged across Ga'Hoole singing and rarely roosting any one place for any length of time. Nestless, they cared not for hollows or the domesticity of life with a mate or rearing a clutch of young'uns. They prided themselves on their freedom, and though at times they were lonely, it was a small price to pay. Actually, they found their lonely conditions to be a great resource for their music and were constantly singing romantic ballads about their nomadic lives and the hope of finding a mate who shared their wanderlust and would never want to settle down or nest.

Faolan shut his eyes, and a deep recess in his mind grew luminous with the glimmer of the Snowy Owl he had once been. Of course, he had not been a male back then. He had been a female whose white plumage was festooned with lacy mosses and the occasional molted feather from a Spotted Owl. How they dressed up back in those days, with strands of bright berries and ice flowers twined in their down! They were all beautiful, but it was their voices that made them legends throughout the kingdoms. At festivals, they sang songs ranging from ach-ingly tender ballads to the liveliest of jigs. The strains of one came back to Faolan, the words twinkling in his mind like light from a distant star.

Fly away with me,
give my loneliness a break.
Fly away with me,
so my heart will never ache.
Fly away with me this night.
Fly away with me,
I'll find a feather for your ruff.
Fly away with me till dawn.
Fly away, then we'll be gone.
Hollows we shall leave behind,
fly to places they'll never find.
Fly away with me right now,
I can't wait.
Fly away with me,
don't hesitate.
I want to soar the smee hole drafts
where the steam rises from the sea.
I want to cross the mountain ridge,
I want to see the other side.

Gwynneth looked at him, for he seemed to have gone someplace else for the longest moment. "Faolan, you'll be fine. I will help you as best I can, but you know . . ." Her voice trailed off.

"I know, Gwynneth."

"Please don't tell anyone."

"I won't."

"And I can still fly. I can feel the wind, you see. That's how I found the eagles — it was their contrails. Owls feel a lot that they don't see. Their gizzards, you know. The impulses that Mrs. Plithiver spoke of, they don't really fade. They are just a bit dimmer." She made a little hop and flew off the edge of the bridge to catch a maverick breeze that had just blown up. "Watch me, Faolan!" she called, and with great delight angled her wings into the night and went into a tail-slide, then flipped over into a flat spin and concluded with a snap roll. Within seconds, she was back on the bridge.

"How about that?" she said triumphantly. "They call them stunts. In the season of the Copper Rain at the Great Ga'Hoole Tree, there was always a big festival, and we'd have stunt-flying contests. Oh, they were fun!" Gwynneth sighed wistfully. "As you well know, not much could get me out of the Beyond to go south to Hoole or the Great Tree, but the stunt-flying contests were irresistible even to a loner like me."

"I bet they were," Faolan said.

"I think I'll go out for a flight now. I'll try and take a closer look at the Narwhale constellation. If I get closer, I think I could count the stars in its flukes."

"Do that, Gwynneth. It would be helpful."

"More than happy." Just as the Masked Owl was spreading her wings to loft into flight, Faolan caught sight of a tail feather she had dropped. It was a lovely tawny color with a few speckles.

"Gwynneth, do you need this?" He picked up the feather.

"Oh, Glaux no, it's just an old feather. It must be my molting season coming on, though who knows what the season is around here."

The Whistler was still on watch with Banja. Mhairie and Dearlea slept with their little brother, Abban, between them, and the two great eagles were perched in the distance on a pressure ridge. Faolan went around the bend to where he had dug out a snow snug with Edme. She was sound asleep with Myrr beside her and Maud as well, since Banja was on watch.

He watched her chest heave rhythmically. She usually slept so her single eye faced up. But tonight it was the crinkled pit of her missing eye that showed. Thin scars raked that side of her face, a testimony to the despicable mutilation wrought by the brutal chieftain of the MacHeath clan. Edme had been born a healthy pup, but she'd been mutilated so the MacHeaths could send a gnaw wolf to the Ring of Sacred Volcanoes. The fur around the wound had never grown back, so the seams of the scars were still deep pink and almost fresh looking. But Faolan saw only perfection. The bone Edme always carried lay beside her with its mystical carvings that seemed to call to something deep in his marrow that he could not quite grasp. He did not worry about that now. He took Gwynneth's feather and tried to imagine what it might look like threaded through the dark gray fur of Edme's ruff. But Edme was a she-wolf who needed no adornment. So he lay it down beside the bone for her to discover on waking.

CHAPTER EIGHT

THE INTIMATIONS
OF EDME

EDME AWOKE FOR NO PARTICU-
lar reason. It was a few short hours before the dawn but
not time for her watch. She heard Faolan breathing next
to her. It was never completely dark on the Ice Bridge,
and a milky light, emanating from the luster of the fullshine moon outside, suffused the interior of the snug. The
snow and ice were perfect reflectors, and the soft light
poured around them. Faolan's silvery coat was radiant
with the reflected moonlight. Every filament of his fur
seemed to sparkle as he slept.

Edme caught sight of a long feather by her bone. It
was mottled with a pale and a darker brown. Obviously, it
was a tail feather molted from Gwynneth, and it had been
placed very deliberately by Edme's side. It had to have
been Faolan who had brought it. Molted feathers did not

simply blow into a snow snug. They couldn't, could they? But why had he brought it? Was it an offering of some sort? An indication that perhaps finally he was admitting to Gwynneth's deteriorating eyesight? Gwynneth and he had spent a great deal of time together huddled at the edge of the Ice Bridge looking at the new constellation — that of the Narwhale. The feather seemed to be a token of some kind, either bearing the burden or the solace of truth. Perhaps it had nothing to do with Gwynneth at all, even though it was her feather. But why had he placed it so that it touched the bone?

She looked over at Faolan. There was something almost ethereal about him in the moonlight. *I am looking for something so deep within him. Something stirs there as he sleeps. Is it a dream? An ancient dream? What is it that I sense about this . . . this old soul within him? What old tunes sing down his bones and lodge in his marrow? I swear sometimes I almost feel a harmony. But what is it?*

She was soon awash in that familiar array of confusing emotions she'd been experiencing since Faolan had first found the twisted femur bone and they had begun this journey to the Distant Blue.

She quietly got up and reached for the bone with her mouth. The scent of the feather was distinct upon it though only its edges had touched the bone. She ran her tongue over the ancient markings and closed her eye. As often happened when she closed her single eye, another eye deep inside her seemed to open. *I need you now*, she thought, addressing the invisible eye. Her old *taiga*, Winks, who also was missing an eye, had told Edme about what Winks called her inner eye, someplace deep in her head, which she described as a kind of spirit eye. Winks had counseled Edme to tend to it carefully, as one might tend to a pup, to nurture and cherish it so it would grow sharper in its vision. Winks firmly believed that it was this inner eye that had guided her back to her own natal clan, the MacDonegals, as a *malcadh*. What was it that Winks had said one of the last times Edme had visited with the old *taiga*? *Be alert, be aware that the eye on your face is not the only eye you possess, my dear.* So Edme clamped her outside eye shut even tighter and concentrated on her inner one.

All the while, she licked the faint incisions on the ancient bone. The Old Wolf words did not seem so strange to her now. She thought that Faolan was the only one to have spoken the ancient tongue, but she now recognized another voice, a very old one. Was it her own? She used to wonder why Faolan had known all these peculiar antique expressions, but now they did not seem peculiar at all. The sounds gathered meaning, infinitesimally small until they began to sift through the pathways of her mind, arranging themselves into phrases that melted out of the edge of her senses. Her hip began to hurt even though she was gripping the bone in her teeth. Usually, if she bit the bone, the pain eased. But this time it was not helping, and the pain grew worse. She knew she must not release the bone. To let go was to let go of meaning. She must try not to cry out, although her single eye leaked tears. But that inner eye, the spirit eye, was dry and clear. Winks's words came back again. *Be alert, be aware that the eye on your face is not the only eye you possess.*

I am alert, she thought through her pain. The eye on her face continued to weep, but she paid it no heed as the inner eye grew wider. She spied a figure hovering over her, a huge silver wolf.

Stormfast, I cannot leave you.

As a Watch wolf, Edme had guarded a volcano called Stormfast, but this wolf was addressing her as if Stormfast were her name. It fit as comfortably as her pelt. Stormfast!

Fengo, you must go on.

Fengo, she thought. Not "the Fengo." It was as if the voices of two consciousnesses, two waking souls were streaming through her mind. But there was little doubt which one it was vital that she hear.

Stormfast, I cannot leave you here to die alone.

No one dies alone, Fengo. You know that better than any. Skaarsgard will be here soon for me.

No! No!

Listen to me, Fengo, my love, we are both old.

I know, I know. I thought I had lost you once and then I fell off the star ladder and came back to you. Now must I lose you again?

You did not fall off to come back to me. You were called back to them — to lead them out of the Long Cold. You will never lose me.

She bit deeper on the bone, and she heard it crack. The dust of ancient marrow leaked out, but the meaning of the gnaw marks on the bone were inscribed on her heart, her mind, and, yes, her own living marrow. She opened her eyes from her waking dream and looked at Faolan, who still slept. The time was nearing when he would know, know from whence this bone came, why it had been carved, and where the other bones remained.

CHAPTER NINE

ONTO THE SEA AND BACK

THE TAILWIND EASING HEEP'S travel arrived just as Faolan's brigade hit a stretch of pressure ridges that slowed their progress to the point that there was little advantage in the wind. In fact, it presented a peril, for each time they reached the crest of a pressure ridge, they were in grave danger of being swept off it.

And so it was decided that the travelers would depart from the Ice Bridge and strike out across the Frozen Sea, where the way was clear and the hard crusted ice would provide swift travel. The eagles would divide their efforts, with Eelon flying out across the vast frozen icescape of the sea to scout for any open water that might threaten to cut channels or leads into the ice on which they traveled. Meanwhile, Zanouche would fly east over the bridge to report on the progress of Heep and his rout.

Edme, however, was adamant about not abandoning the Ice Bridge entirely.

"I don't think it's wise, Faolan. We should travel out across the sea at night when the winds blow the hardest and it is the most dangerous to cross the pressure ridges. With the wind backing around to the northwest and east, it will give a tremendous boost to our speed. The nights have been clear, and the stars are brilliant, so you will be able to guide us. But most important, we will always be able to find our way back to the bridge." She paused and stepped so close to Faolan that their noses were touching. "Promise me, Faolan, on your marrow: If the night is thick with clouds and there are no stars, promise me we will not leave the bridge?" Edme sounded almost desperate.

Everyone else, however, had been terribly excited about leaving the bridge, if only for periods of time. Faolan could not quite grasp why Edme was so reluctant. There was an impulse in Edme that seemed to be driving her fear of the open ice. He must be patient with her.

Near the end of their first night abroad on the Frozen Sea, the creatures were ecstatic with their progress. Gwynneth reported that they had avoided almost a half a dozen pressure ridges by taking the sea route. As they neared the pillars of the bridge, Eelon swooped down with a small seal in his talons.

"Where did you find that?" Banja asked.

"Abban told me how to hunt for them before we left at dusk."

"Abban?" Caila said. And they all turned and looked at the wolf pup. His ears twitched.

> *My paw did see. For ears it has.*
> *And tiny rustlings in the ice.*
> *They sound just like little mice.*
> *I tap once, they tap twice.*
> *I know their breath holes can't be far.*
> *Closer than the nearest star.*

A truly preposterous bird flew out from under the Ice Bridge. It had a large chunky orange beak that seemed to grow from its face like a strange chubby flower. Its head was black except for two large white discs on either side in which rather small eyes were set. Its cheeks billowed voluptuously, giving it a clownish appearance. The feathers of its chest were pure white, but its wings and back were black.

"Greetings and salubrications."

"No, it's 'salutations,' idiot, not 'salubrications.'" A large group of the creatures waddled up.

"Are they birds?" the Whistler whispered.

"Of course we're birds, you fool. Ask your little friend there," the first bird replied, nodding at Abban.

"Oh, yes indeed, they're birds," Abban replied.

"And?" asked the Whistler.

"And what?" replied Abban.

"You always speak in rhymes — what happened? I thought you were going to introduce us. And you just stopped," the Whistler said.

"I can't think of anything to rhyme with 'bird' except 'turd,' and my mum would be very angry if I said a disgusting word like that."

The bird snapped its beak in excitement. "Little friend, you just said it! 'Word.' 'Word' rhymes with 'bird.'"

"Yes, I suppose you're right," Abban answered.

"So we're wordy birdies. How about that?"

"Except you're puffins — huffin' puffins," Abban replied.

At that same moment, Gwynneth landed on the ice.

"Puffins! I don't believe it," she exclaimed. "I haven't seen any since the Ice Narrows. I never thought you came this far west."

"Is this west?" one puffin asked.

"I guess so, Dumpkin," replied the other.

"Dumpkin?" Gwynneth said. "That's your name?"

"So they tell me," Dumpkin, the female, replied.

"It's just like the Ice Narrows," Gwynneth said. "Nine out of ten puffins were called Dumpy."

"Yeah, well, we didn't want to take the same name. A little diversity. We've —" The female puffin paused. "We've EVOLVED!" She hopped up and down. "How do you like that, Dumpster? Talk about big words! I call 'evolved' a fifty-capelin word."

"Dumpster?" Edme asked.

"Oh, yes, forgive me. My manners!" She giggled maniacally. "This is my hubby."

"Hubby?" they all said.

"Yeah, it means mate," Dumpkin said. "It's an old word."

"Old Wolf?" Dearlea asked.

"Are you kidding me?" Dumpkin replied. "No, it's an old word left over from the Others."

It was as if icicles had run down the animals' spines.

"Yeah, you know, the Two Legs." Dumpkin glanced at Gwynneth and Eelon. "Present company excepted. I mean the two legs without wings. The Others."

Abban slowly approached Dumpkin and Dumpster and sank to his knees, then tucked his tail.

"Oh, sweetie pie. You don't need to do all that," Dumpkin said. "You want some fish, of course. I don't know how you've stood those lemmings for all these days."

Her hubby waddled forward. "I'm surprised you haven't turned into one — lemme tell you!" Dumpster said with a chuckle.

"Oh, great ice!" Dumpkin roared. "You are so funny." She threw herself on the ice and stuck her feet up in the air while batting her wings. "That is a knee-slapper." The bird convulsed with laughter. "Oh, oh, oh, oh" was all she could utter while she rolled around on the ice. "A knee-slapper! Lemme tell you, lemmings — get it?"

"We don't have knees, Ma!" a third and somewhat smaller puffin cut in.

"Oh, Dumpette!" Dumpster exclaimed. "Did you hear my joke? 'Lemme tell you' I said — like, they are sick of lemmings. Do you get it?"

"Yes," she sighed, and flicked her eyes shut as if one more second of these insufferable parents was going to drive her to do a head dive through the ice.

"A real knee-slapper."

"But as I said, Ma. We don't have knees."

"Oh, so we don't!" Dumpkin rolled back onto her feet. "All this time I was trying to slap my knees. No wonder I couldn't. Well, Dumpette, our friends here are hungry for something other than lemmings." Dumpkin began to giggle again.

"Pull yourself together, Ma," Dumpette said. Her voice was thick with boredom.

"No!" She snapped her orange beak. "You pull yourself together, dearie. Hustle those tail feathers and get out there and start diving. These dear, sweet animals need some fish — capelin to go with that seal."

"All right, Ma." Dumpette gave her mother a withering glance but shot off into the air and could soon be seen diving under the ice.

"I'll go, too, sweetie," Dumpster said.

"Bye-bye, Dumplings!" Dumpkin waved her wings. She turned to the others. "Adorable, aren't they? I actually love it when Dumpette gets sassy. She didn't do it this time. She was just plain bored. I prefer sassy to bored. That bored thing she does is so . . . so . . . boring." She sighed. "Oh, well, kids will be kids." She sighed again, then waggled her wings. "I'm going to go out there and help my Dumplets fish," she announced, and spreading her wings awkwardly, she lifted her plump body into flight.

The blood from the seal stained the ice. The sun rose behind them, casting a pink hue over the bridge and silhouetting the chunky forms of the puffins against the dawn.

"What is it?" Caila asked her pup. Abban stepped forward to look at the puffins diving for capelin.

"Line them up one by one, then eat them in the rising sun!" Abban chirped.

And that is exactly what they did. It was a feast that morning. The fish were rather small, perhaps a quarter the size of a salmon. They were of a drab greenish color, except for their sides, which were shaded in silver and white. Their bones amounted to nothing, and they were salty on the tongue.

"Amazing they can do anything with such tiny bones," the Whistler commented. "I'll have another if there's enough."

"Oh, plenty," Dumpette replied.

"Do we have to eat the eyes?" Myrr asked.

"The eyes are the best part, dear," Dumpkin said. "Quite delicious. Soft, but when you first bite into them they bounce around a bit in your mouth. Just chew them up. Yum!"

In no time at all, their bellies were full.

Soon they fell into the habit of finding good places to sleep during the morning hours, the winds from the previous night persisting in fitful gusts until midday. They would rise just after noon and, with new energy, tackle the pressure ridges ahead. Then at night, when the wind rose again, they would climb down one of the massive sloping pillars of the Ice Bridge and slip out onto the Frozen Sea and make their way toward the Distant Blue.

When they slept in the mornings, they always posted a guard. On the first watch of this day, Mhairie and Dearlea walked the boundary lines of their encampment.

"Mhairie, have you thought what it might be like when we get to the Distant Blue?" Dearlea asked.

"How do you mean?"

"It has to be different in so many ways."

"I know. New stars, new . . . new hunting formations maybe."

"Does it worry you, Mhairie?"

"Of course it worries me. I was trained as an out-flanker for a *byrrgis*. If there are no *byrrgises*, what shall I do? In this new formation that Edme calls the Fortress, we're all outflankers, more or less."

"But if there is game, big game not lemmings, there will have to be *byrrgises*."

"I hope so." Mhairie's voice almost cracked.

"I'm afraid of something, too," Dearlea said.

Mhairie stopped pacing. "What's that?"

"You forget."

"Forget what?"

"I was chosen as the next *skreeleen*. But we have not had a *skree* circle since we left. No stories have been howled. It's been more than two moon cycles now."

"But . . . but . . . it's all been so hard, so different. Getting here to the Ice Bridge and then the pressure ridges and Abban falling into the sea and coming back *cag mag*. There has hardly been time for a *skree* circle. Everything has been hard."

"When has it ever been easy for wolves? Tell me that. Don't you see, Mhairie, if we don't keep telling the stories, we shall forget them. And if we forget them, our marrow will leak away, our clan marrow will vanish."

"We don't have clans now. It's hard to think of clan marrow the way we used to."

"Then, what are we on this bridge?"

"We are nine wolves, three pups, two bears, an owl, and now two eagles," Mhairie replied.

"Is that not a clan of sorts?"

"I suppose so," Mhairie conceded.

"Clans have stories. Clans make stories. Will there be

stories to tell in the Distant Blue? Will any creatures want to listen? There was so much we had to leave behind." Dearlea's voice dropped off. "I hope stories are not among them." She gave a great sigh, then muttered something that was barely audible.

"What did you say?" Mhairie leaned in closer.

"Nothing," Dearlea murmured. Her tail drooped, her ears hardly flickered. She felt lost in some storyless place where *skree* circles seemed as odd as puffins. Where words disappeared or were reduced to just a few. Would they become like the puffins, who could only think of names that all sounded alike? Were those preposterous-looking birds really so dumb that they had lost their ability to name things? If language was swallowed by the unknown, the vastness of the unknown, if things could not be named — then there was no hope. Dearlea was a namer as much as Mhairie was a hunter, an outflanker. What would she do in this new world?

CHAPTER TEN

HOWLS OF
A MAD WOLF

ZANOUCHE WAS NOT AS YOUNG as she used to be. Her hearing had dulled, and the roar of the wind did not make it any easier. The wolves from the Outermost, Heep's rout, were huddled beneath the overhang of a pressure ridge. A fierce gale was blowing, and clouds seemed to slide down from the dome of the dark night like boulders. Zanouche flew over the lip of the ridge. Turbulence did not faze her. With her immense and powerful wings, she could negotiate any draft. Lightning cracked the sky, and the electric veins of white sent a shudder through the wolves.

"It's a curse . . . a curse," a wolf below her howled.

"By my tail, it ain't no curse!" Heep's voice scalded the night. "I'll get her back. I'll get him back, and when I do — Lupus, when I do — I'll kill her before that pup's eyes. That will show him."

Show him what? Rags thought, but dared not speak the words aloud. Rags, a large red wolf, slid his eyes toward the yellow wolf as he staggered onto a promontory. *A mad wolf, that one*, Rags thought.

Heep braced himself against the wind and turned his head toward the moon, which seemed to blink as clouds raked across it. His eyes took on a reddish glare. In the moon's inconstant light, he began to howl his imprecations and foul curses, always waving the tail that had been restored to him during the time of the Great Mending.

How I would love to bite that tail clean off, thought Rags. Had not Heep's mate, Aliac, whom Heep now cursed, threatened just that when she had left with the pup? If Heep was not mad before, her leaving had driven him to a level of insanity that made the wolves of the rout quake with fear. And now they were alone with Heep on an Ice Bridge to nowhere. They knew not where they were going, just that they were headed away. They had no name for what was ahead.

Rags was certain that Faolan's pack knew their destination. For Heep's rout, this journey was a quest for vengeance — no matter where it took them. Vengeance was all the yellow wolf thought of. Vengeance flowed through Heep's veins and hardened his marrow.

"I'll find you, Aliac and Faolan. I'll chase you into the perditious flames of the Dim World, where the *vyrr-wolves* tend the hearths. The *grot* boils in my blood and quickens my marrow!"

Rags had seen many awful things in his life in the Outermost, but for the first time, he was truly frightened. As he watched the mad wolf bellow at the moon, it was as if a trickle of light had seeped into his head and illuminated his brain. *He will lead us to our death because of his vengeance. He is as blind as an old wolf with the milk-eye sickness, this one. As dumb a brute as a musk ox.*

From a past he could not quite grasp, dim memories came to Rags, memories of wolves with craft and true cunning, wolves who hunted in *byrrgises* and not the savage *skelters* of the Outermost. He shivered with loneliness.

Zanouche glided high above Heep, wondering if she could swoop down and pick off this wolf. He wasn't a large wolf, really. Larger than a coyote, yes, but she and Eelon had killed coyotes by picking them up, flying high, and then dropping them on hard ground. Usually the coyotes died instantly. If not, they were so broken that she could make short work of them. Could she and Eelon take care of this soulless creature together?

But what would that solve? Surely another one of these savage outclanners would rise up to take his place. Would that wolf be as poisoned with hate, as consumed with revenge as this yellow one? And if that wolf was as mad, would she and Eelon have to kill him as well? This bridge was the only link between the old world of the Beyond and the new one, the one that Faolan and his followers called the Distant Blue. She and Eelon had appointed themselves protectors of Faolan and his friends. They wanted to help this brave brigade of animals find their way to the Distant Blue.

Zanouche remembered the first time she had ever seen Faolan, when she was flying high above the river in the Beyond. He was but a yearling then. She had watched surreptitiously as his grizzly Milk Giver had taught him to swim. There was something about him at the time. Even though he was young, he seemed to have an inherent nobility. When she had returned to the home nest in Ambala, she told Eelon about the pup.

You say his pelt is silvery? Eelon had asked.

Yes, bright as the moon, she had replied.

And he has a turned paw?

Yes, I saw it when he clambered out onto the banks.

This is astonishing! Eelon had exclaimed.

Absolutely astonishing. He was swimming with a huge grizzly who was caring for him as if he were her own cub.

Not astonishing in that way, Zanouche.

What do you mean?

I flew over that pup when he was on his tummfraw. I could have picked him off.

Most of the animals in the Beyond had, at one time or another, taken an abandoned wolf pup set out to die. At the end of the hunger moons especially, it was a common practice to feed on *malcadhs*.

But you didn't take him. I remember now. You said you sensed something about him and you just flew on.

Yes, and now you've seen the same pup. He's alive!

Most definitely alive, Zanouche had replied.

And now this horrendous wolf Heep and his rout of savage wolves were out to destroy Faolan and his followers. But Zanouche wondered if she and Eelon were the gatekeepers to the Distant Blue. Who were they to decide who could come into this new world? Suppose one of the wolves in that contemptuous rout of sheer savagery had the possibility of becoming perhaps not a noble wolf but a decent one? Perhaps deep in its marrow a strain of righteousness and fairness might lurk. Was it up to Zanouche and Eelon to decide who could proceed across this Ice

Bridge to the Distant Blue? There was something unseemly about their making such decisions. Or so it appeared to Zanouche.

She looked down. The yellow wolf was frantically whipping his tail in the wind. His howling scorched the night. The clouds had cleared off, and the full moon blistered the sky with its whiteness.

CHAPTER ELEVEN

STARSIGHT

THE CLOUDS HAD BEGUN TO ROLL in thickly. The puffins started to cluck and squawk as they became increasingly unsettled throughout the morning, and then Dumpette, who had been out on a scouting flight, skidded into a somersault landing on the Ice Bridge and squawked, "Storm coming! Storm coming!"

"When?" the Whistler asked.

"Now, maybe, or later —" She paused and blinked several times. "Or in between perhaps."

"That's, er, helpful," the Whistler replied.

"Hole up, that's what's helpful!" Dumpette squawked.

And so the brigade holed up, and it was none too soon. From their snugs in the pressure ridge, they peeked out to see the storm advancing like a solid gray wall of slashing rain and sleet.

"It's going to be a wet one," Edme said. They could all smell it in the air. Somewhere far out there, the Frozen Sea had melted and the roiling winds had sucked up moisture from the open water. It struck fear in them. Wet meant warm, and what would happen if the Ice Bridge began to melt?

The storm reached its greatest intensity on the evening of the second day. The wolves dared not stick their noses out, but despite the slash of wind and ice, the puffins always managed to bring them fish. They thoughtfully placed them within a paw's grab, so the animals would not go hungry. The birds would always leave a few extra fish for Abban. They seemed inexorably drawn to him and his odd ways.

The wind howled incessantly, and more than once, the travelers thought they heard the sound of cracking ice. During the night, they heard a terrible snap. It was the kind of snap that reminded them of the snap of a caribou's spine when they brought it down. Except this was a thousand times louder. Faolan and Edme both sat up straight, their ears shoved forward, their hackles raised.

"What happened?" Edme gasped.

"I'm not sure!" Faolan replied.

There was the unmistakable voice of a puffin outside

the den. The orange beak of Dumpette poked in from the darkness. "Don't worry. It's just an iceberg hatching."

"There're icebergs out there?" Edme gasped.

"Yes, they break apart when the weather gets warmer. We call it hatching."

"B-b-but . . . but . . . if the weather gets too warm, this *mhuic* bridge might hatch." Edme's swearing, calling the Ice Bridge crow scat, was surprising. She rarely swore. For her to hurl an imprecation at the bridge that she never seemed to want to leave was extreme.

"Oh, the bridge has been here forever. It would take forever for it to melt. You need not worry about that. Come spring, it gets a bit slippery and little pieces might break off here and there, but it's nothing to bother you."

"Little pieces here and there!" Edme screeched. "What if we are on one of those little pieces?"

"Hush, Edme!" Faolan said. "A shriek like that is enough to split ice. Do calm down."

Edme suppressed a growl. She hated it when someone told her to calm down. She glared at Faolan until he laid his ears back and sank down into a submissive posture.

"Sorry," he mumbled.

Edme immediately felt terrible. She hadn't meant to hurt Faolan's feelings, but even though she only had one eye to glare with, she'd been harsh and sent a hurtful message.

"No, I'm sorry," she quickly replied. "We've just got den fever I suppose. How long have we been shut up here? Three days?"

"Just two."

"It seems like forever," Edme said.

They would be stormbound for another two nights. They dared not venture out of their den, let alone onto the Frozen Sea, where the starry maps of the night sky were obliterated by roiling dark clouds. Each evening, Faolan poked out from the den just far enough to scan the sky for those four extraordinarily bright stars on the Narwhale's tusk, but he could not catch the slightest glimmer of them.

The winds that had been behind them before the gale had turned yet again, and now they presented a barrier as solid as any pressure ridge. The puffins advised the wolves move their camp to the base of the ice pillars. There were snugs down there, and the pillars themselves offered more protection from the wind. Thus the wolves took refuge beneath the bridge, huddling in snugs between two ice pillars, the very same ones that the puffins used to roost in. But the adult wolves were driven half *cag mag* by the puffins' incessant chatter and terrible jokes.

The pups and the cubs found the birds endlessly amusing. Abban did not laugh out loud as the others did, but appeared to enjoy some sort of special relationship with the puffins that made him quite content with their babble. As Edme pointed out, he seemed to have such a special bond with all sea creatures that he even whispered what sounded like a little prayer before eating one of the many capelins that the puffins brought them daily.

"Look at him, Faolan," Edme whispered as the pup bent over the dead carcass of a silvery olive-colored fish. "What's he muttering?"

"I guess giving thanks to the fish for giving up its life."

The Whistler blinked in astonishment. "You mean *lochinvyrr*? He's actually performing *lochinvyrr* for a fish that is already dead? *Lochinvyrr* is for the dying, not the dead."

Lochinvyrr was the ritual that wolves followed when a prey they had brought down was breathing its last. It was a demonstration in which the predator acknowledged that the life it was taking was a worthy one. But in this case, Abban was not the predator. The barely weaned pup had not killed anything in his life yet. His mother, Caila, did the hunting, and until recently, she had even chewed up the raw meat of the lemmings and regurgitated it for her pup to make it easier for him to digest. But here he was performing *lochinvyrr* for a dead fish.

"It's quite irregular, I agree," Edme said quietly.

On the fourth day, when the puffins had just brought in their last load of capelin, the gale began to break. The sun was rising and splinters of light bounced off the bridge. It was still too windy to begin traveling in their Fortress formation on the bridge or to travel on the Frozen Sea.

Eelon arrived with Zanouche. The two eagles alighted at the base of the ice pillars.

"It's still blowing like stink out there," Eelon said. "But in a few hours it should be good for travel."

When they set out later, everyone seemed enthusiastic except for Edme. Faolan glanced at her. *What is it with her?* he wondered. She always seemed to want to stay on the bridge. Yet the way was so much easier out on the sea, even when the winds were sweeping across it. Faolan could tell her hip was not improving, that it was possibly even a bit worse. The bone she carried seemed to help some, but not enough. He felt the seeds of dread begin to take hold in his gut.

"I have an extra capelin if you'd like, Faolan," Banja said.

"Oh, I'm not really that hungry. You take it, Banja."

Edme looked around. *Now what's wrong with him?* Faolan never passed up food.

By dusk, the wind had died down and was barely a riffle across the ice. Soon the last of the setting sun's colors vanished behind the Distant Blue, the sky became very black as the moon had dwindled since they had been stormbound, and the stars broke out. There were great clusters of them unfurling like hot white banners in the night.

"There he is!" Faolan exclaimed.

"Who?" asked Edme.

"Beezar. He's back. Remember, we hadn't seen him for a while. Look I can clearly see that first star in his stumbling paw. Now, what is that star's name?"

"I don't recall there was ever a name for that star," Edme replied.

"Oh, yes. Yes, there was. . . ." Faolan looked up at the star that twinkled with a slightly pink glow. "I think, I think it was Kil —"

"Kilyric," both he and Edme blurted out the name at

the same time. They swung their heads toward each other in stunned amazement.

"Where did that come from?" Faolan asked.

"It's an Old Wolf word," Edme said. But the sound was so familiar to both their ears, and the word didn't feel old at all.

"See, Edme, you know more Old Wolf than you ever thought."

Edme felt her marrow quicken. She had been carrying the bone under her chin but shifted it and gripped it harder between her teeth. Had the word come from the bone? Now more than ever she wanted to stay close to the Ice Bridge. Had she not known better she would have thought there were flakes of strong rock metal embedded in the ice, for it was as if the bridge were pulling at her. But she knew Faolan would not want to return. They were traveling fast. What little breeze stirred the air was with them.

Faolan was completely absorbed with the stars of Beezar and Kilyric and then sighed joyously as the starry tusk of the Narwhale appeared. "You see, Kilyric is pointing the way. We just keep it slightly to starboard and then the tusk of the Narwhale to port and we won't lose our way to the bridge or the Distant Blue." He tipped his head up and spotted the Masked Owl. "Gwynneth! Gwynneth!" he called excitedly. "I spotted the star in the port forepaw of Beezar. Beezar's back."

Gwynneth flew straight up and out ahead of the brigade. Squinting into the starlit night, she thought she almost saw it. She knew her vision was deteriorating, but if a star was bright enough, she could usually get a fix on it. It took her a bit, but finally, it came into focus. She was thrilled. Between that and the very obvious stars in the tusk of the Narwhale, she could navigate now. She carved a broad turn and came sweeping back in.

"Faolan, keep the tack you're on. That's two points off the paw star of Beezar, so you are between it and the first star of the Narwhale's tusk. You'll go true." She hesitated. "I think . . ."

"You think what?"

"You know the star we owls call NeverMoves?"

"Yes, I've heard you speak of it."

"Well, I think we have found the NeverMoves star for this world. It's Kilyric."

"But it's in Beezar's paw. Beezar moves," Faolan said. "He was gone for several nights."

"Yes," Gwynneth replied. "He was gone for bright nights when we could have seen him. I thought perhaps he was one of the many things we had to leave behind. But I think he was near, very near. He stumbles, you know, and maybe he blinks just a bit when he stumbles. And when he blinks, the star in that stumbling paw dims. But it's still there. You'll find it, Faolan. It will become easier and easier for you."

"How?"

"Because you have a kind of starsight."

"Starsight? What do you mean?"

"You understand the stars and how to navigate."

Edme tucked the bone in her mouth back under her chin. "You do, Faolan. You have it. What Gwynneth says is true. Starsight. I've always known it."

"Always?" Faolan asked, turning to her.

"Always." She hesitated. "But can we get back to the bridge at the first streak of dawn?"

"Yes, of course, Edme. I promised."

He knew there was a reason for this impulse of Edme's not to leave the Ice Bridge. He sensed that she was not quite sure why she must do this. But one never could really explain impulses. One could only trust them. And he trusted Edme like no other wolf in the world.

Dearlea had been trotting not far behind the two wolves. She had watched them standing in a pocket of moonlight, carefully discussing the new star in the paw of an old wolf, a wolf from the skies of the Beyond. The star stirred her imagination. Why had they never seen it before? Was what Gwynneth said true? That when the old wolf stumbled, he sometimes blinked, and in the blink of Beezar's eye, the star might have dimmed? It sounded like some old legend, and that was what excited her. It was a new legend. No *skreeleen* had ever sung of this star, Kilyric. The very name sounded like a song to Dearlea. A melody came into her head, and with it words, words to be howled by a *skreeleen*.

> *Oh, where do we go in this land of ice?*
> *Oh, where do we go on this star-swirled night?*
> *We go west with the sun*
> *West with the light*
> *Until it dips down so far out of sight*
>
> *The Distant Blue is said to be there*
> *But who is to know and who is to care*
> *Except for the blind and stumbling wolf*
> *We follow his star prints into the dawn*
> *And hope that the next night the track is not gone*

Kilyric is our great hope
Our prayer and our song
Oh, Lupus let not this star be gone
Gone over the bright flashing rim of the morn
To another world not yet born.

How can the blind lead the seeing?
How can the deaf hear the song?
How can the pup — a fool — sense the way?
How can a wolf read the stars in the sky?
How can we know if we'll live or die?

League after league on this lonely sea
Where is the star ladder, the Cave of Souls?
For beneath us a watery grave does roll.

Beezar, Beezar, show us the way
The star in your foot we will follow
Blind in our trust to get to the morrow.
To the Distant Blue — who knows what waits
What time will bring and what might be our fate.

"Dearlea, what are you muttering? Don't tell me you're going *cag mag*, too?" Mhairie said, drawing up next to her sister.

"I was just humming really. The tune is an old one." *The words are new*, Dearlea thought, but did not want to say. "Didn't you recognize it?"

"One of those Old Wolf things?"

"No, it's not that old. It's one that Alastrine used to howl."

"Alastrine?" Mhairie said vaguely. "I haven't thought of her in . . . in . . . I'm not sure how many moon cycles. But you shouldn't be thinking about Alastrine out here. Think about trotting. We're making good time. We're going so fast — there's no time for idle thoughts, sister."

But where are we going, really? Dearlea wondered. *And how much have we left behind?*

Dearlea had to fight the urge to turn right around and run as fast as she could back to the Beyond. Back to where the *skreeleens* once sang their stories. Back to the Ring, where the Watch carved tales and legends into bones.

CHAPTER TWELVE

SPIRIT FAST

IT WAS THEIR FOURTH NIGHT OUT on the ice since the storm. A sliver of moon was just rising, and Faolan looked back over his shoulder to check their position in reference to the forepaw of Beezar, which was just clawing over the horizon. Again there was little wind, and the surface of the Frozen Sea was hard and smooth. Zanouche had reported that Heep's rout was having difficulty. One wolf had died when the winds had kicked up and he had been scraped off a ridge. Another had gone missing and was presumed dead. This was all good news.

From behind came a strangled little yelp. Suddenly, Edme was beside him.

"What was that?" he asked.

"Abban! Something's wrong with him. He's having a fit."

The two wolves raced to where Caila stood transfixed over her pup. Abban was flat on his belly and seemingly insensate but writhing. His eyes had rolled back into his head. He was barking but not in singsongy verses. Faolan had never seen anything like this and wondered for a second if Abban had been struck with the foaming-mouth disease. Abban's mouth was not foaming, but there was blood. He had bitten his own tongue.

"Quick, give me that bone, Edme," said Faolan.

She didn't think twice but instantly dropped to her knees and shoved the bone between Abban's teeth.

"Abban? Abban, what is it?" she cried. But Faolan suddenly knew. He pressed his once-splayed paw hard against the ice, and he felt the same vibrations that Abban was experiencing. He looked up and spied the tusk of a narwhale.

"Urskadamus!" he cried. "Old Tooth. He's come to warn us. There's a lead opening up."

They heard it, and next they saw it. The horrible cracking sound as if their own spines were splintering. A fissure of water opening up, slithering toward them.

"Run!" Faolan howled.

"Attack speed!" Mhairie called out in the voice of a seasoned outflanker.

Immediately, Abban seemed to recover. He was up and streaking toward the Ice Bridge like a small comet.

Edme ran like she had never run before. *Lupus get us to the bridge. Lupus!* She was frantic. They were all frantic, but Edme alone knew that if the sea swallowed her she would not only lose this life, but another. She must get to the Ice Bridge to find that life, that . . . that — *gyre?* What a strange word. But it was the right word. The right word for what she had lost and was about to recover.

"Maudie!" A shrill, agonized cry came from Banja, who had been running right behind Edme. "Maudie, she's drowning!"

Edme's mind went blank. Slowly the words dropped into her consciousness. *I cannot run. . . . I must go back. . . . I promised Banja to . . . to . . .* Moons ago, when they were still in the Beyond, she had promised to look after Maudie if something happened to Banja. Could she keep running away toward the Ice Bridge if it meant Maudie was lost? Edme knew what she had to do. She felt a sob break from her throat, but Edme reeled around and raced back to where Banja was swimming in the opening of the crack. "I can't find her. She bobbed up once and I tried to grab her, but a wave washed us apart. The lead, it just swallowed her."

Without thinking, Edme plunged in. She clamped her mouth shut tight. The cold was shocking, but she was numb to pain. If only she could become numb to the terror, the thought of little Maudie sinking to the bottom and her own terror of the ice closing the lead completely and being trapped beneath it. Where was Old Tooth? He had saved Abban. Could he not save Maudie?

Edme knew how to swim. She had swum all the time in the north branch of the great river in the Beyond. It was the only place where a gnaw wolf could find food.

But it was different with so much ice around. She had a strange, suffocating sensation that any minute she might become confused, disoriented, swim off in the wrong direction and become locked beneath an ice grave.

The lead had widened. She saw something glimmering back up the channel, where a current flowed away from the bridge. It was two strange-looking creatures, similar to Old Tooth but white as alabaster and with no tusks. Oddest of all, they swam not on their bellies but straight up in the water. Between them, they held a sodden little lump — Maudie! They floated beneath her so her head was above the water. She could breathe!

Great Lupus! thought Edme. Something beneath her rammed Edme hard, and she was flung from the water. As soon as she landed, the two luminous heads rose and, as gently as a mother setting down a pup in the whelping den, set Maudie on the ice beside her. They said nothing, but they nodded as if to say, "Follow us, walk beside us to the end of the lead, and you'll be safe." So Edme took Maudie in her mouth as if she were a whelping pup and followed the two pearly white whales. The narwhale led the way with his tusk.

It was not like with Abban. Neither Edme nor Maudie came back speaking gibberish. They were clear-sighted, clearheaded, and able to recount exactly what happened when they had reached solid ice and climbed back onto the bridge. Banja pressed her shivering wet pup to her flanks, but Maudie didn't stop talking. "Oh, Mum, they were so nice and their skin so smooth and polished. And they just held me up and they made these funny little soft sounds between them and then the narwhale made little tooting noises."

"What were they saying?" Myrr asked.

"Well, I'm not really sure. I mean it wasn't a language

I could understand. There were just these soft airy little puffs and snorts. But I think the narwhale, the one Faolan said was Old Tooth —" Maudie broke off to glance at Abban, who merely nodded. "I think," Maudie continued, "Old Tooth was showing them the way through the lead to where the ice was thicker and they could set me down. They held me all the way with my head above water. Imagine that! They are so smart. They know that we can't breathe underwater." She paused. "I'll never forget the touch of their skin."

Myrr stepped forward. "Was it like a night during the Moon of the Mossflowers, when the softest air blows down so lightly that it hardly stirs the petals of the mossflowers? Was that what their skin felt like?"

"What nonsense!" Edme barked. The travelers all turned to her in surprise. They were unaccustomed to Edme snapping in such a surly manner, especially at Myrrglosch, the pup she had practically raised.

"Myrr, may I remind you, and you" — she nodded at Maudie and Abban, who stood nearby — "that not one of you pups has ever experienced a summer in the Beyond. The last true summer in the Beyond was almost three years ago, when not one of you was born. You've never even seen a mossflower. Let alone this nonsense about what they might feel like on some . . . some" — she began to stutter — "mythic summer night."

Faolan blinked. This outburst was so unlike Edme.

Myrr stepped up. "But we can imagine, can't we? Just because we can't see something, can't touch it, doesn't mean we can't feel it."

Edme closed her eye briefly. Her heart raced. She knew what Myrrglosch said was true. Why did she want to deny him a bit of fanciful thinking and denounce the pups' imagination? What could be worse than disdaining imagination? Without it, they might never have survived the famines, never escaped the torn lands of the Beyond. Was she worried that Myrrglosch, a fearless little wolf, was dangerously attracted to this sort of adventure? Even the cubs seemed enthralled with Maudie's tale. She wanted to curse that *mhuic* sea.

The brigade settled down for the rest of the night in a snow snug on the bridge and planned to set out again at dawn. Eelon had reported that there was only one pressure ridge on the bridge and it was not exceedingly high. However, several leads had opened up on the Frozen Sea and traveling on it would be impossible for a while. Edme took great comfort in that news. She was about to leave for her watch when Faolan came up to her. Her tail drooped, and she began to sink into a crouch of submission. Faolan lowered his own tail as well. He couldn't stand to see her like this.

"I know I spoke wrongly. I was . . . was . . ." Edme stammered.

"I came to thank you, Edme, not to scold you." Faolan winced. One did not scold an equal. One scolded a pup.

"Thank me?"

"You saved Maudie's life. You saved it at the risk of your own life. No one thanked you."

"Banja did. Oh, she did, Faolan. There's been such a change in her since she became a mother."

"Well, I think you have some mothering to do now as well?" She looked up at him. Confusion swam in her eye.

"Myrr — go back, comfort him, Edme."

"I know. I was awfully sharp with him, wasn't I?"

"A bit. He'll get over it."

"It's just that I worry. This sea." She looked out at it. "Pups and cubs, the young ones, they all crave adventure in a way I don't think we ever did."

"We were gnaw wolves. We had enough adventure just surviving."

"But we are just surviving. Trying to get to the Distant Blue alive, isn't that enough adventure?"

"Yes, one would think so, but the difference is that as gnaw wolves we were always living on the edges of a pack, of a clan. We had no family to keep us safe. This little brigade of ours has become a family — we are a clan."

"Yes, I suppose you could say we are a clan of sorts."

"No, not of sorts, Edme." Faolan's voice hardened. "Make no mistake that we are a clan. The first clan in this new world of the Distant Blue."

Edme returned to the snow snug and Myrr lifted his head.

"Edme, are you angry with me?"

"No, dear. Never. I was wrong to speak so, so harshly."

"But it was my fault, Edme."

"What? No, not ever. Why would it ever be your fault?"

"My stupid imagination," Myrr said, and Edme inhaled sharply. "Imagination can be bad. I know."

"What? What are you saying?"

"My mum and da, they imagined the prophet was real. They thought he was Skaarsgard, come down from the star ladder to save them. They joined the Skaars dancers. And it was all in their imagination — even when you and Faolan showed them who the prophet really was, they wouldn't believe you. That's what I mean. Imagination can be very bad."

"Imagination can be good, Myrr. If we can't imagine, we cannot feel another creature's pain or sadness. Imagination is why we do *lochinvyrr* — to tell the dying animal we understand its pain, to thank the animal for the sacrifice of its meat."

"Sometimes I imagine the saddest thing. I imagine . . ." Myrr's voice dropped.

"What is it, Myrr? Tell me, and maybe it will help."

"I imagine that maybe, maybe I might do something bad and you'll turn your back on me and walk away like Mum and Da did."

Edme reached out and pulled the pup close to her. He could feel her heart beating just as he had when Edme and Faolan had taken him over the crest of the pressure ridge. "Listen to me, Myrr. That is never going to happen. I cannot even begin to imagine that. We are not blood kin, marrow kin, but we are kin in a way that is unbreakable."

"Like paw fast?"

"Not exactly, because I am much, much too old to be your mate. But let's say we are spirit fast."

"Spirit fast. I like that."

"Well, we are." And Edme hugged the pup closer. Myrr felt her heart beating, and he knew his world was complete.

CHAPTER THIRTEEN

"ABIDE AND HE SHALL GUIDE!"

THEY WOULD NOT VENTURE BACK onto the Frozen Sea for several days. The leads had fractured the ice into a deadly maze, and they were confined to the Ice Bridge. They could look down and see pools of water between large fragments of ice. The puffins could fish closer to their ice nests in the bridge.

Fortunately, the pressure ridges were much flatter than the earlier ones, and this made the passage easier. If they could not find snow snugs on the bridge itself, the pillars beneath offered refuge. They became inured to the incessant chatter of the puffins, who continued to bring them capelin. Often in the evenings, during the time they would usually go out onto the ice, Faolan would go to the edge of the bridge and scan the myriad leads for any sign of tusks, looking for Old Tooth, who had twice saved their lives. Things were changing. The winds blew warmer and the ice was shrinking and the water expanding. The puffins said the bridge had been here forever. But Faolan knew things were never forever. The Ring of Sacred Volcanoes had collapsed within one night. Could not the same thing happen to this bridge? *What is the meaning of forever? Forever is for the dead*, Faolan thought. *Not the living.*

An ice floe not far from the bridge seemed to be dissolving before his eyes.

One evening at twilight, as Faolan was watching from one of the ice tongues that projected from a pillar and offered a perfect platform for viewing the seascape, Edme came up beside him. She knew that he longed to be back on that frozen plain.

"You miss it, don't you?" she spoke softly.

"It's not missing it exactly. I just feel that there is a whole world beneath that we know nothing of, creatures who are so different from us. Imagine, Edme, if there were life on the stars, on the moon — doesn't it make you want to see it? And Old Tooth, who is he? What does he think? Why does he help us?"

"Abban seems to know somehow."

"Yes." Faolan drooped his head toward the water. Suddenly, he jerked. "Did you see that?"

"What?" Edme asked, but then she saw it — flashes in the shallow water. Like flames from a pale fire, the cobalt blue water surrounding the ice pillars began to pulse with light.

"It's them," said a small voice. Abban appeared between them. "I knew they would come."

They? Edme wondered. Then a group of creatures broke through the surface and lifted their heads from the water. They were the same whales that had rescued Maudie, rolling in the shallows near the pillars as if they were scrubbing themselves. Abban began to tremble, and his eyes widened in horror. Faolan was about to ask him what was wrong, but then he saw. One of the whales had been raked, and blood oozed from the wounds on his skin.

"My father's fangs, my father's claws!" Abban howled.

"Great Lupus!" Edme gasped.

"How would Heep dare come so close to the water to attack such a creature? The outclanners are so fearful of water."

The Whistler broke in. "But Heep was raised in the Beyond, not the Outermost. He can swim. Perhaps they are starving and were driven to the water's edge in search of food."

Zanouche's call suddenly scratched the inky sky.

"Heep! It's Heep."

There was a great stirring in the air overhead. Zanouche and Eelon melted out of the night and alighted on a fragment of ice that bobbed near the pillars. The two eagles were out of breath from their flight. Zanouche began to speak.

"I had lost track of them for several days."

"Where are they now?" Edme asked. The rest of the travelers gathered behind Faolan.

"An ice tongue had formed beneath the bridge between pillars in a long span you crossed over maybe half a moon ago. They traveled underneath, and we couldn't see them. But they're getting closer fast."

"Faolan! Listen to me," Caila implored. "We have to get away, now! Heep, he's . . . mad. He'll kill me. He'll kill Abban!"

"If only the ice were solid," Zanouche said. "They're fearful of the Frozen Sea. They would never venture out on it. They don't understand the stars. They're fearful of losing their way."

The creatures all looked toward the sea and saw the

huge leads that had opened up and the pale blue ice floes dotting the water.

"Why, I wonder, is the ice blue?" Faolan mused aloud.

How can he be talking about the color of icebergs at a time like this? Edme thought.

"It's similar to why the sky is blue," Gwynneth said, alighting beside him and seemingly ready to indulge him in his musings. Of course, Gwynneth had known Faolan longer than any of them, including Edme.

"How is that?" Faolan turned to the owl.

"The blue light scatters instead of being absorbed," Gwynneth replied, as if this was a perfectly normal conversation to be having. The rest of the brigade was on the verge of growling with impatience, and Toby stomped his feet. "Some say that the very oldest icebergs are the bluest. I'm not sure about that. It could be that there are more air bubbles in the younger ice. The famous sage of the Great Ga'Hoole Tree, the Spotted Owl Otulissa, lived for many moons in the northern kingdoms, doing research on such matters."

"Very interesting," Faolan murmured, and then turned to regard the cubs.

Edme, an even-tempered wolf, was ready to explode. *What is he thinking? Why is he blabbing on about the color of ice when Heep was fast on their heels?* She felt a cold chill run up her spine as she watched him observing Toby and Burney. The cubs had grown much, much more than the wolf pups. They now stood twice as tall as the wolves.

"Toby, Burney, you know how to swim, don't you?"

"Of course. We lived by the river. We swam as soon as we walked."

Faolan remembered his own swimming days that first summer with Thunderheart. Bear cubs learned to swim earlier than wolf pups. So Toby and Burney would be fine.

"What are you thinking, Faolan?" Edme asked apprehensively.

Faolan was standing very still with his eyes clamped shut, but in his mind, an image stirred. Faint echoes came to him from an ancient bone he had carved and was now buried in the cairn of the Fengos back at the Ring of Sacred Volcanoes. The strangest thing was that, despite the destruction wrought by the earthquake and followed by the rampaging glacier from the north, the bones of all the chieftains of the Watch had remained unscathed. And Faolan saw in his mind's eye the bone that his first *gyre* soul etched upon his arrival out of the Long Cold into the Beyond. The bone depicted wolves leaping from ice floe to ice floe.

Wambling! Of course! That was the name for what they did. The Ice Bridge had become impassable. They were forced to go out on the great chunks of sea ice. They had leaped from floe to floe, and when the distances became too great, they swam.

Faolan turned toward the brigade. "We can do this. We can swim and we can jump. Heep will never follow us."

"But the pups?" Banja, Edme, and Caila all spoke at once.

"We'll get them across — floe by floe," Faolan replied. Then Abban spoke up:

Swim I can. Swim I am.
Paddle, paddle paw and tail.
I know the way,
I shall not fail.

Caila cocked her head to one side and peered at this strange son of hers. She said not a single word, but her questioning expression said everything. *But how, Abban? I never taught you.* There was a rueful mist in her eyes as she wondered how this little defenseless pup had learned something without her. Had he been laid open to dangers when she was absent? It was a wistfulness for moments lost — lost and irretrievable. She stepped closer and ran her muzzle through her son's withers.

All pups loved it when their mothers muzzled them. It felt so good to have their mothers' warm, damp noses poke through their pelt to their skin. Abban loved it, too. He just didn't exactly know if his words would come out right when he spoke them. So he remained silent. He knew that while she was muzzling him she was casting bitter glances at Airmead. Why was she this way now with the white wolf?

Airmead, who was a large wolf to begin with, seemed unusually big because of her color. But she appeared to shrink. Her jaw quivered, and her tail dropped. Abban felt sorry for her. His mother hadn't treated her this way before his fall into the sea. Was there something he did not understand about the white wolf?

"But what about Maudie and Myrr?" Edme asked. "They're so tiny. Their legs aren't long enough to leap. They can't swim."

"Don't worry, we'll do it," Faolan replied. He was about to say, "We did it once. We'll do it again," but he stopped himself. They would not understand. "It's called *wambling*."

"*Wambling?*" the Whistler asked.

"It's an Old Wolf term." Faolan began to stammer a

bit. "It . . . it . . . it was inscribed on one of the history bones at the Ring of Sacred Volcanoes."

"Really, Faolan?" Edme tipped her head a bit to one side as if trying to recall.

She had just begun to grasp the meanings of Old Wolf, but there was something elusive about this one, *wambling*. And what was this history bone he referred to? Edme had no recollection of it.

"Don't worry, Edme. We can do it." Faolon looked at Maudie and Myrr. "Eelon and Zanouche can help the little ones."

"Of course we can," Eelon said.

"We'll carry them," Zanouche added, then looked Myrr up and down. "You're not as big as a vixen."

"A female fox?" Myrr asked huffily.

"Oh, I meant no offense, dear," Zanouche said. "You're ten times as smart and much more handsome."

"Of course I am. Males usually are more handsome," Myrr replied.

"I'll let that go," Zanouche said with a slight whiff of indignation.

"Now, how do we do this?" The Whistler came up beside Faolan. He seemed genuinely enthusiastic, more so than the rest.

"Well, first you slide down this pillar's ramp!" Faolan stepped onto where the pillar met the top of the bridge at a gentle angle and was soon at its base. Then he made a leap into the air. It was a classic high-arcing scanning jump. He landed gracefully on a sheet of floating ice bobbing nearby off the bridge. "And then you try for the next!" he announced.

They all held their breath, for the closest floe was at least four times the distance of the one he had just landed on. "But you're a Watch wolf, and so is Edme and Banja. You're used to performing great leaps and jumps. Dearlea, Caila, the Whistler, and I aren't," Mhairie cried out.

"Mhairie!" Caila snapped. "I raised you as your second Milk Giver. And I am a turning guard and you an outflanker. You have muscles. And so do you!" She nodded at Dearlea. "And you, too, Whistler. You can do it. You can learn to do it. If you miss, you know how to swim. It's the pups I worry about. But if the eagles help —"

"Oh, we shall! We shall!"

"Well, then, we have nothing to fear. For I'll tell you, Heep will never follow us out there. Never!" She turned to Abban. "Abban, tell me truthfully. You really feel you can do this?"

Yes, Mum, yes!
Swim I can, swim I am
And look forsooth
Here comes Old Tooth!

They turned and the swags of pearly light seemed to part to make way for the narwhale plying his way between the ice floes.

"Abide and he shall guide!" whispered Abban.

CHAPTER FOURTEEN

A Dim Memory
Comes Back

THE GLASSY SEA WAS UTTERLY
still. The moon was dwindling to No Shine, and there
was barely a sliver left. But it was a cloudless night, and
the stars were bright. Rags, crouching under a pillar perhaps a quarter of a league behind the brigade, could not
believe his eyes. Wolves were leaping from ice floe to ice
floe. Sometimes he caught their reflections mirrored on
the black water. How could they do it? How could they
dare to do it? Of course, some of them were from the
Watch at the Ring of Sacred Volcanoes and learned to
leap, but others had never been on the Watch and they
were doing it. However, what was most incredible was
that little Abban, Heep's son, was swimming — actually
swimming between floes.

Rags began to tremble. He knew he could never do
that. But would it be worse than living with Heep's rout?

Still, he didn't know how to swim properly. None of the outclanners knew how, for there was very little water in the Outermost. The river where most wolves in the Beyond had learned to swim did not run through the Outermost, and there were no lakes. The outclanners dreaded water more than anything. The Ice Bridge seemed safe to them. The vast expanse of ice that had blanketed the Frozen Sea in the beginning of the journey was a comfort. Heep had even begun to plant the notion in the rout that there was no water beneath the ice. It simply didn't exist. Heep, of course, would say anything to get the outclanners to follow him. He had big dreams for himself in the new place they were going. He would form powerful clans. He saw himself as a Chief of Chieftains. But what would he say now? Now that the ice had peeled back in so many places to reveal a deep green sea.

Rags himself had no such dreams of becoming a chieftain. His only hope was to survive. He thought of this new land as a place to reinvent himself. The longer he had been away from the rout, from the Outermost, the easier it was to retrieve some of his first memories. He had been the youngest of the last litter of his mother, who was quite elderly when she gave birth. All of the litter had died, except for Rags. His mother was not a particularly warm wolf. She was in fact rather vain and hardly paid any attention to him. One day, she announced that she had found a second Milk Giver for him. She was too busy to contend with nursing a young one. "My days of running a whelping den are over!" she had announced, and set off with a handsome black wolf who appeared to be much younger than she. But the second Milk Giver complained about him drinking too much milk and not leaving enough for her own pups. So again he was shoved out of the whelping den.

Rags was not sure when he had first noticed the strange-looking wolf following him. It was a she-wolf, and to call her hideous would not have been an overstatement. She was as ugly as his own mother had been beautiful. Her mangy pelt was thick with burrs, and the fur stuck out every which way, as if caught in a perpetual gale. She was rough to look at from afar, but up close she was worse. She had one eye that skittered about as if it might bounce out of its socket at any moment. And when Rags dared to look more closely, he could see that the other eye was a different color. Nevertheless, she seemed concerned about this motherless pup, and when Rags was cast out by his second Milk Giver, she set about to find him a third. And she did. It was a gray wolf who had been cast out from her clan for giving birth to a *malcadh*. The *malcadh* had been taken from her and put on a *tummfraw* to die as was decreed by wolf law. But the she-wolf's breasts were still heavy with milk.

"Oh, Sark," the grieving mother sobbed. "I'll try. I'll try."

"You'll do fine. I know he's not yours, but the milk will bind you to each other."

"I didn't even get to name her before the Obea took her."

"That's sometimes better, dear. But this one you can name. Look. He's a strong little fellow. What might you call him? Let's think of a name."

"Oh, I can't," the she-wolf moaned.

"I'll help you. Now, let's think. You come from the MacNabs, don't you?"

"Yes, ma'am."

"There was a wonderful *skreeleen* down there — oh, it was many years ago — but he told these stories about a wolf, a handsome fellow called Ragmore. I believe he had distinguished himself in a battle where wolves of the Beyond had gone to the northern kingdoms to help the owls. Some time ago. But he was brave and valiant and there's even a flower up there that blooms on the edges of avalanches that they call Ragbloom in his honor. They used to sing a song about it, but I can't recall it now."

"That does sound like a nice name, a lovely story. Ragmore — it's a very nice name," the she-wolf said.

Little did any of them realize that the newly named Rags and his third Milk Giver would only have the briefest of time together. For it was just hours after the disreputable-looking but kind wolf had left and Rags, full of milk, nestled against the belly of his third Milk Giver that he heard a scuffling sound outside. A strong odor penetrated the den. Suddenly, a claw sliced through the darkness. His Milk Giver screeched, and Rags leaped from her belly. Blood flew through the air. Rags tore out of the den and slid into a rocky crevice to watch in horror as an animal much larger than his Milk Giver emerged from the den, dragging her body out. Her throat had been slashed, and her dangling head was attached to the rest of her body by only a few bloody tendons.

The murderer caught sight of him. With milk still wet on his muzzle, the pup knew he would now die. He had suckled from his last Milk Giver. But the horrible creature, which he would later learn was a wolverine, looked at him and merely yawned. It was as if Rags was too small, too insignificant to even bother to kill.

Rags, full of milk and full of fear, began running. He ran and ran, fueled by those deep draughts of milk he had been drinking for the better part of a day. He had been fed, and he had been named. Perhaps that was enough. For the next several nights, he hid out in the tiniest dens, lodges, and rock notches he could find, places where nothing as large as that horrible creature could reach. It was spring. The weather was fine. There was no milk, but quite honestly, he had given up on milk and Milk Givers. He quickly learned how to kill the smallest creatures, such as fox kits, when their mums were absent from the dens, or take the eggs from unguarded ground nests of birds like ptarmigan. If he had to, he killed the mothers. Finally, he arrived in the Outermost. Milk was but a dim memory. The fur on his muzzle was now stiff with blood. He vowed never to think of Milk Givers or mothers again.

Sometimes, however, he thought of that disheveled, disreputable-looking wolf. His third Milk Giver had called her either ma'am or Sark, a strange name. Of course, once he got to the Outermost, the vision of her raggedy pelt swirling with burrs did not seem so odd. None of the out-clanners were groomed. They always appeared wild and savage, and the stink of blood was high on them since there was scarcely a shallow creek to bathe in and they were so fearful of water.

But, nevertheless, despite her unkempt ways, the Sark

had differed in a very significant way from the outclanners. She was kind and spoke the language of wolves so beautifully. The outclanners hardly spoke at all. Words seemed as foreign to them as water was to the Outermost. Rags had never really thought about this until now. Their language was rough, and it was always about the present, never about the past, and they did not have the kinds of minds that could plan for the future. This trek was the perfect example. When Faolan and his followers departed for the Frozen Sea, Heep and his rout could go straight, for they had the course of the bridge to follow. But they were not really that good at anticipating, planning, or strategizing like the wolves of the Beyond with their hunting *byrrgises* and intricate schemes for bringing down big game like elk and moose.

Whatever happened to the Sark? Rags thought wistfully now of the strange she-wolf. She was a nice creature, despite her hideous appearance. Then he thought of his first Milk Giver, who was so beautiful but whose milk might as well have been poison. Was there any hope for one like himself? Rags wondered. Any hope at all? Perhaps in this new land, this nameless land, there could be.

CHAPTER FIFTEEN

WAMBLING

SO THE WOLVES OF THE BEYOND
and the bear cubs, along with the owl and the two eagles,
did abide as Abban had counseled. Old Tooth guided
them from floe to floe. The Whistler, Caila, Mhairie, and
Dearlea soon were making short leaps. But Faolan, Edme,
and Banja, all veterans of the Watch, would take the floes
two or three at a time. In scraps of moonlight, their shadows reflected on the unusually calm waters of the sea,
which appeared almost glassy. Faolan, arcing high into
the air on his leaps, saw the constellation of Beezar mirrored on the water's surface. The star Kilyric blazed in the
stumbling paw. *I must name the others*, Faolan thought.
*The other stars in Beezar's foot and those of the new constel-
lation of the Narwhale.* For he realized in the instant
between leaping and landing that to be a namer of things

was as important as being a navigator, a star wolf. They were going to a world that was new to his friends but old to him. And there must be names. Old Wolf was a lovely language, but the old needed the new in order to truly come alive. It was through words that things became real. Language could draw minds into a compact with reality.

At the very same moment that Faolan was thinking about words, so was another wolf. Dearlea was surprised at her own capacity to leap. She couldn't take the ice floes two at a time like Faolan, and for the ones that spanned a greater distance, she swam and was often gently nudged along by Old Tooth or one of the pearl whales, who watched over them with all the vigilance and concern of mums on their pups' first ventures out of the whelping den.

The narwhales were fairly silent, but these pearl whales made a great number of noises as they traveled. There might be a rush of clicks followed by a resounding clang reminiscent of a Rogue smith's hammer striking metal and then a series of whistles. And although Dearlea did not understand their language and the whales could not speak to her, she felt as if they were communicating. She was wrapped in their songs and wondered if whales also had *skreeleens*. Sometimes she could almost grasp the meaning of their clicks. She even sensed that the other animals in their brigade felt the sea creatures' songs as well. Sometimes the narwhales bellowed low, lovely phrases into the night, as if they were cheering when one of the wolves would make a daring leap or one where their reflections shimmered on the still dark waters of the sea. Dearlea was determined to remember every moment of their adventure abroad on the breaking ice of the Frozen Sea.

I'll tell you a story you might never believe
It happened one night on a vast frozen sea
Where the water meets ice
In a gentle wind's lee
We jumped in the darkness
Beneath sparkling stars
From floe to floe we leaped
Guided by tusks of the nars.

Sometimes we would swim
And then I would hear
The songs of the pearl whales
As they began to appear
I did not know a word that they said

But the melody did wind
Through my head.

Their songs seemed to tell
Something deeply true
It matters not your kind
You can be born anew
The wolf that never leaped
The pup that never swam
Can dare what they never
Dreamed on the land!

These creatures from the deep
Gave courage we never knew
But every song they sang
We felt it so true.

Though their songs were made of words
We did not ever know
They gave us the gall grot
To leap from floe to floe.

CHAPTER SIXTEEN

ICE ROT

ANY TEMPTATION TO GET BACK to the bridge diminished one night as they settled on a floe when the moon was exceptionally bright. They were startled to see long shadows sliding across the bridge.

"It's Heep!" Caila had shrieked. "That tail! That cursed tail!"

Indeed, the immense shadow of a wolf's tail swept across the bright moonlit ice of the bridge. And so they stayed out for another several nights and made good progress. Zanouche and Eelon assured them that Heep's rout had encountered several very tough pressure ridges and was now quite far behind. But their time on the open sea was growing short as the distance between the floes had increased and the ice floes began to shrink.

"Faolan," Edme said one morning as they rose from a floe that was barely large enough for the two of them.

"I know. I know. We have to get back to the bridge," he responded quickly.

Edme was relieved that she did not have to say anything more. The moment the decision was made, Old Tooth appeared. He seemed to sense exactly what had to be done. He began to swim through a new lead that had formed just before the dawn. The floes were small, unable to support more than a single wolf at a time, but the passage provided the most direct route back to the bridge. They all had one thought in their minds — to outpace, outdistance, to get as far as they could from Heep. He could not follow their trail, for their tracks had vanished from the bridge a half moon before.

But Faolan knew that no matter what, Heep was a survivor. The madness in his marrow, his taste for revenge, was what nourished him. Zanouche had disclosed the wild rants she had witnessed from Heep on the crest of the pressure ridge.

"When I think of it now, it still gives me tremors," Zanouche said.

"What did he say exactly?"

"Exactly?"

Faolan nodded.

Zanouche sighed. "He said, *I'll get her back. I'll get him* back, and when I do — Lupus, when I do — I'll kill her before that pup's eyes. That will show him."

There was a long silence after Zanouche had finished.

"We care about you, Faolan," Eelon said. He swung his magnificent white head around. The gaze from his small, hard eyes seemed to penetrate deep into Faolan's marrow. "We care about all of you," he repeated.

"We always found you wolves fascinating, but we are shy birds. Fierce but shy. However, over these moons, we have felt a bond grow between us," Zanouche added.

"Yes indeed — a bond," Edme echoed. "That's so true."

"We had often flown over the Outermost. We've seen this yellow wolf. Heep is like a disease."

"He's dreadful enough! I'll tell you that," Edme barked. Heep had a well of hatred in him that was as venomous as the poison of the foaming-mouth disease.

Faolan turned to her. "Try not to be anxious, Edme. By my star calculations, I think we shall be nearing the end of the bridge soon. We cannot be that far from the Distant Blue."

She didn't want Faolan to be consumed with worry about her. He had others to care about. More important things to worry about. Edme gave a soft chuckle to distract him.

"Do you suppose that when we get nearer, we can stop calling it the Distant Blue? Perhaps we could call it the Near Blue."

"Maybe we'll have to come up with a completely new name."

"I suppose that would be practical, but I rather like the sound of the Distant Blue. It's a bit poetic, don't you think?"

"It is," he agreed.

"Does the meaning always have to match the reality of a thing?"

"I'm not sure." Faolan tipped his head to one side and thought. He had supposed if the meaning and the reality of a thing were always identical, matched up precisely, it might not allow for poetry, for the music of language. The *skreeleens* told stories, legends that they had certainly embellished over the years, yet the truth of them seemed to shine through.

Almost as soon as they stepped onto the bridge, they knew something had changed in the texture of the ice.

Ice rot! The words exploded in both Faolan's and Edme's brains as the surface crumbled wetly under their paws. On the river in the Beyond, they had experienced this as the time of the spring moons drew closer, when they were winter thin and dared to look for fish. But there it was not so frightening. The river was not nearly as deep as the Frozen Sea, and the shores not too distant. If they did break through, they could clamber out onto a nearby bank. The ice holes they fished were never far from shore at that time of year.

The moon that brought the unstable ice had been called the Moon of the Cracking Ice. It was a time that was always welcomed in the Beyond with great joy, for it signaled the end of the hunger moons. There were festivals to celebrate the return of the herds. It meant that the *byrrgises* would start forming up to follow the meat trail.

The Cracking Ice Moon was the very first of the spring moons. The second was the Moon of the Singing Grass and the third was the Moon of the New Antlers. But it had been more than two years since they had seen any of those moons, felt the slightest warm breeze riffle their pelts. They had instead entered a cycle of endless hunger moons.

The irony of their situation on this Ice Bridge struck

them. For so many years, they had yearned for spring, and now it might be their destruction. If the bridge collapsed and the ice floes shrank to the size of small ice boulders, what would they do? There was no recourse. They were still hundreds of leagues from the shores of the Distant Blue.

Spring at last! What a cruel joke it was. For here, spring signaled doom.

"You don't know," Banja said as she came up to them. "There could be another freeze."

The Whistler was beside her. He was pawing the surface ice. "A paw's length down it seems quite solid," he said. "I say we keep going as fast and as steadily as we can."

"Will the pups be able to keep up?" Edme asked.

"I can carry Maudie," Banja said. "She's such a tiny thing."

Toby and Burney suddenly appeared. "We're big," Toby said. "Look how big we've grown." He stood up and pumped his forepaws into the air. "It's nothing for us to carry pups on our backs, or by our mouths. The same way our mother carried us."

Faolan's marrow suddenly stirred. He remembered so clearly his first spring. Thunderheart had often grabbed him by the nape of his neck with her mouth and carried him about. His feet would dangle just above the ground. When he had grown a bit bigger, he had begun riding on her shoulders. It had given him a wonderful view of the world.

"Yes, we can do this. We'll proceed at press-paw speed," Faolan said.

"We'll cut our sleep by half," Edme spoke up for the first time. They looked at her, somewhat surprised.

"You really think so, Edme? You think we can do that?"

"Yes. As long as food is not halved, we'll have the energy. There are lemmings, and the puffins keep bringing us capelin."

"And the cod, my God, the cod!" Abban burst out.

"What is he talking about?" Dearlea asked.

The pup scampered off to the base of one of the ice pillars. They watched as one of the pearl whales swam up to where the pup stood and slapped a large speckled gray-green fish at his feet. The fish was so large that Abban could hardly handle it by himself, and the Whistler ran out to meet him. "I'll help with that, Abban. What a fine pup you are!"

The fish tasted very different from the small ones that the puffins brought them. Not as salty but much meatier, with firmer flesh.

"This is the closest we get to real meat," the Whistler commented.

"What do you mean by 'real meat'?" Katria asked.

"You know — caribou, elk. Of which I might add that as a gnaw wolf I only got the scraps. So you most likely know real meat better than I."

"I would have to agree. This seems more substantial than those tiny boneless fish," Katria replied.

"Yes, but the bones are bigger, so be careful," Faolan said. "They're just big enough to choke on, but not to gnaw." Faolan continued in a thoughtful voice, "That's the one problem with fish, I would say. Their bones are . . . are sort of soft. You can't get a real grip on them, and to try and make a design on them would be impossible."

"No, they couldn't sustain a design at all," Edme said, chewing on a piece of cod tail.

"Thus sayeth the two gnaw wolves of the Ring!" the Whistler winked his eye and spoke in a jolly tone, but Faolan and Edme were both suddenly overcome with a yearning for those long winter nights when the She-Winds blew and they were off duty. They would take a bone, a good bone, to where a Rogue smith might have set up a forge, and gnaw a lovely design while the owl went to work with hammers and tongs and created something beautiful out of a lump of metal. Those were special times. It seemed almost impossible now that they had spent evenings, often until the dawn broke, just making art!

"Look!" Mhairie said. She turned toward where the pearl whale had delivered the cod. The water was boiling with the silvery gray-green fish. There were hundreds of them.

"It must be their spring run, just like the salmon in the Beyond," Faolan said. But the very sound of the word "spring" sent jitters through their marrow.

The pearl whales had slapped several more cod on the pillar base, but the brigade had eaten its fill so they started out again at press-paw speed.

"I'm not going to be carried in your mouth, Toby," Myrr protested. "That is completely humiliating. I am a weaned pup!" He stomped one paw and wagged his tail vigorously.

"Then ride on my shoulders," Toby replied.

Abban, who had fish scales glittering in his muzzle, stood in front of Burney. "I care not how you carry me. As long as I can see the sea."

Burney swung him atop his shoulders as well. Maudie scrambled onto Eelon's broad wings, where she had traveled when they flew over the ice floes. She was quite content and found that the feathers under the primaries were as soft as the fur of her mother's belly. But what she loved most was the view. With her claws hooked over Eelon's broad shoulders, she could peek out from behind his head and see everything.

On a clear day, the Distant Blue seemed real, not just a place the grown-ups talked about. "It's just a band of color," Eelon had said on that first day. "But every day does it not seem thicker and darker? Soon we'll see solid land."

"You'll see it first, Eelon, and you, too, Zanouche." Gwynneth was flying abeam of them. "Eagles' eyes are sharper than wolves' or owls'. It won't be just blue then. You'll see land, true land!"

True land. The thought sparkled in Maudie's brain. "Do you think there will be trees and lakes and forests and mountains?"

"Where did you get those ideas, Maudie?" Gwynneth asked.

"I've heard my mum talk about such things and you as well, Gwynneth. You've been every place — the island of Hoole in the Sea of Hoolemere. You've seen the Shadow Forest and Silverveil, where your auntie came from. And what's that place where you come from, Eelon and Zanouche?"

"Ambala. A lovely forest it was!" Eelon's voice became rueful. "We lived in an ancient nest that belonged to Zanouche's great-great-great-grandparents Elver and Zan, very good friends of King Soren." He sighed. "But all that is gone now. We need a new place now, a new landscape."

"With new creatures?" Maudie asked.

"Possibly," Gwynneth replied.

"I want friends," Maudie said in a small voice. "Friends who look a little bit like me maybe and speak the kind of words we all speak."

"You mean the language we speak?"

"Yes. I don't understand any of that fish talk. Abban understands it, but I don't." She paused. "And there's one other thing I hope there's not."

"Something you hope won't be there?" Gwynneth asked.

"Yes."

"And what might that be?"

"Gnaw wolves."

"Gnaw wolves? But your mother was a gnaw wolf and at one time so were Faolan and Edme and the Whistler."

"I don't mind if a wolf is born looking funny. Poor Edme — her eye never healed like my mum's. But they shouldn't be called gnaw wolves and made to feel separate and awful so other wolves beat them up."

"I don't think that will happen, Maudie. We are going to a new place. Our old ways won't work. We must invent new customs, new laws, new ways of doing things."

Though her vision was dim, Gwynneth looked at the little pup who seemed even tinier somehow on the massive wings of the eagle. *Who was Maudie's father?* she wondered. Maudie had a deep reddish pelt, redder than her mother's, which suggested that the father must have been red as well. The offspring of a red wolf who mated with a silver or a gray or a black wolf were usually "mud pelts," the term for the dull brownish hue of their fur. Well, the color of Maudie's pelt or who her father was did not matter, but there was no arguing that Maudie was an uncommonly intelligent pup. It was more than wondrous, Gwynneth supposed, that she had been born in a time of famine.

CHAPTER SEVENTEEN

OLD WOLVES IN NEW PELTS

THE DAYS GREW LONGER. THE COD delivered almost daily by the pearl whales were rich with tender flesh. The animals felt themselves get stronger each day and were able to continue at press-paw speed. The pups were growing and soon capable of walking on their own for long distances, with only occasional breaks to be carried by the cubs, who seemed to have tripled in size, or the eagles. This meant that Eelon and Zanouche could resume flying out on scouting missions to track Heep. But so far there had been no sightings, even though the eagles were careful to fly under the bridge.

With the spring moon, the ice would often melt during the day, leaving great puddles on the bridge, and then refreeze at night. But the new ice was not that solid. It was "rotten," as the wolves called the spring river ice in the Beyond. Their paws slipped and broke through to the puddles that still lurked beneath. And it was hard to discern a track, for no footprints could be left in puddles of water.

No one spoke the thought out loud for fear of jinxing their most desperate hope — that Heep and his rout had somehow met their end.

Dusk was falling when they came to what appeared to be a fork in the bridge. Both Zanouche and Eelon had flown out ahead to scout the two forks and see if one was more passable than the other.

"They both rejoin again within less than a league. From the air, they looked the same," Zanouche said. Eelon nodded in agreement.

"What looks the same from the air can differ when on foot," Edme said. "And now with this sea fog rolling in, it will be hard going."

"Mhairie and I can scout," Dearlea volunteered.

"No!" Edme snapped, then immediately apologized for her tone. "It's just that I can take the north fork and Faolan can take the south."

"Alone?" the Whistler said.

"Yes . . . yes, alone," Edme said. There was something in the manner in which she spoke that let them know she would brook no objections.

The Whistler looked at his old friends as they walked off. He had known them a long time. He knew their ways from the time they were all young gnaw wolves together, competing at the Gaddergnaw Games. As he watched them disappear into the twilight, he knew that this was no mere scouting mission but a very private journey for each of them. In some way, it was connected to the Cave Before Time, where he himself had spent so much time as a member of the Blood Watch. The paintings in the Cave were deeply linked to Faolan, and, he now realized, probably to Edme as well. That bone she carried had been found in the cave.

The Whistler watched them both as their paths diverged at the fork. This private journey was one that might not be so much of distance covered but time recovered. The two wolves seemed to him like outriders. Yes, that was what they were — outriders of time. It was not the terrain underfoot that concerned them, not the possible pressure ridges or the melt water on the bridge, but the folds in time. The Whistler thought of the old tale that the *skreeleens* often told, the story of the Ice March out of the Long Cold that first brought the wolves to the Beyond. It began with the chieftain who had reached the moment of *cleave hwlyn*, the moment when a wolf's body separates from its soul and the soul begins to climb the star ladder. Only in this story, the chief was called back to lead his clan out of the Long Cold and his soul had tumbled from the star ladder. *And now*, thought the Whistler, *what are we doing but coming out of another Long Cold on another Ice March, but from the opposite direction? It is all reversed. We have come to a fold in time! And those two know it.* But the Whistler sensed something else. It was not merely time that was being folded. Two lives were folding in on each other. There was, he knew, a profound bond between these two wolves that had defied time. It could only be called love.

The pain in Edme's hip worsened with each step, but she had to get to the place. That was what she called it in her mind — just "the place." She could think of no other word. She reflected on the fact that she was a *malcadh* made and not born, and therefore had no *tummfraw*, the spot where *malcadhs* were abandoned to die after birth. But she had a sense of this place. If *malcadhs* were lucky enough to be selected to serve on the Watch, they had one last task before going to the Ring. They were told to seek out their *tummfraws*. This journey was called the *Slaan Leat*, a journey of forgiveness, a journey toward truth. But for Edme, it had uncovered a terrible lie — that she was not a real *malcadh*, but had been mutilated at birth by her vicious clan chieftain.

The journey that Edme was on now was her true *Slaan Leat*. She walked the north fork to another site of abandonment, where as an old wolf she had elected to be left behind, begged to be left. Her own deformity had been concealed for years. It did not show like those of *malcadhs*. Hers had been a slightly twisted femur that had grown worse and more painful with age, but never impeded her until the Ice March out of the Long Cold. *Oh, my,* she thought, *I am truly a very old wolf. Thousands of years old.* And now with each step, she was drawing closer. The ice was becoming soft, and yet there did not seem to be puddles. In fact, some rocks had become exposed, and a filigree of tiny lichens spread across them. She wondered briefly how a rock could become embedded in the Ice Bridge. If the bridge had been made by a moving glacier, all sorts of things could be rolled into the ice, from rocks to uprooted trees. But she did not wonder about this for long, because she suddenly knew that she was very near. Her heart beat wildly, her marrow shivered. Her hackles bristled straight up. She shut her single eye, and, feeling her legs crumple, she slid down to the rock surface. It was almost warm from the afternoon sun, as if it had saved the heat just for her. "I am here," she whispered. "Here!"

It was not a *tummfraw* that Edme had arrived at — quite the opposite. It was her place of *cleave hwlyn*, the place where, centuries before, her soul had separated from her body, the place of her death. And now her heart began to slow, but she knew it would not stop. For she was not dying, but only entering an ancient dream. The story of the twisted femur that she had gripped in her mouth across the Crystal Plain onto the Ice Bridge was becoming clear.

Leave, leave now, dear Fengo!

I can't leave you here to die, Stormfast.

In her sleep, Edme blinked — blinked, it seemed, with two eyes. For Stormfast had been her name and she'd had two eyes then.

My soul is pulling away. Skaarsgard is coming for me.

She spoke these words in her dream to Fengo.

And Fengo replied: *He came for me, then cast me from the star ladder. I didn't come back only to lose you again, Stormfast.*

You didn't return for me. You came back for the family, the teaghlachen, *to lead them out of the Long Cold.*

But I can't do it alone, Stormfast.

Fengo, I promise you will not be alone . . . ever . . . ever . . . Slaan boladh.

Slaan boladh were the last two words that the wolf named Stormfast spoke. Their meaning in the language of Old Wolf was clear — "until the next scent post."

On the other fork of the bridge, less than a quarter league away, Faolan, too, had fallen into a strange waking dream. His eyes were wide open. He stood very still and he experienced a kind of cleaving — not the cleaving of death but life, the life of his first *gyre*. A year had passed since Fengo had led the family, the *teaghlachen*, on the Ice March out of the Long Cold. Faolan's first *gyre* was looking for something. But what was it? He squinted harder into the mists. *What does he want? What is he looking for?* Faolan wondered.

It was as if the spirit of his first *gyre* and his last *gyre* had comingled. *Why is the old wolf weeping? Why am I weeping?* Overhead, an owl was flying. It was Grank, the Spotted Owl, Fengo's dearest friend. He was leading him somewhere. Suddenly, Fengo's hackles rose. He caught it — a dream mark he had left, one of the special scent posts that wolves leave to indicate where a mate or a pup had died. At the same moment, he saw the Spotted Owl begin a steeply banking turn. He was spiraling down toward a scattering of bones. Faolan began to race toward that spot, his legs a blur.

"Here are her bones," called Grank. It was Grank who had come with him to revisit the *drumlyn* he had made in honor of Stormfast. Now Fengo sought to retrieve just one bone to carry back to the Beyond, to the Cave Before Time.

Fengo looked down. Through the scrim of his tears he saw the bones, scrubbed clean and white by moons of the year since the Ice March out of the Long Cold. It was as if they were waiting for him. His eyes came to focus on one bone, one single bone — a twisted femur.

Faolan had first seen that bone in his dreams four moon cycles before, on the eve of the earthquake. And two moon cycles after that, he saw it for real, not in a dream but in the Cave Before Time. It had lain glistening in a spike of moonlight. He had called it the loveliest of bones and had been inexplicably drawn to it, drawn to it like the flakes of metal to strong rock.

He was not conscious of walking, or even moving, but suddenly, Faolan found himself on the other fork, the one Edme had taken. He saw the shape of a wolf curled in sleep. The bone was still gripped in her mouth.

He looked down at her. "Stormfast," he whispered softly. The sound of the name was a welcome one. It had been so long since he had spoken it aloud. She rose up almost immediately. Her hip pain was gone!

"I told you, Fengo," she replied.

"You told me what?"

"*Slaan boladh* — until the next scent post." Edme paused. "And here we are — old wolves in new pelts." She chuckled softly. "With new names — Faolan and Edme."

"Can we become paw fast again?" Faolan asked. He cocked his head and looked deeply into her single green eye. His ears twitched nervously.

"But, Faolan, we were always paw fast." She nuzzled him behind one twitching ear.

He stepped back and looked at her with such earnestness.

"I mean now, on this Ice Bridge, in our new pelts and with our new names. Will you, Edme, who was once Stormfast, for whom the volcano at the Ring was named, take me as your marrow mate, as your paw-fast wolf? For I, Faolan, now in my last *gyre*, but who was once in my first *gyre*, Fengo, take you forever and ever, Beyond the Beyond and into the Distant Blue and, when the time comes, unto the Cave of Souls."

"I shall. And now I, Edme, in my second *gyre*, but who was once the she-wolf Stormfast, take you, Faolan, forever and ever, Beyond the Beyond and into the Distant Blue and into the Cave of Souls, as my paw-fast mate."

The two wolves put their paws together. First Edme put hers atop Faolan's, then Faolan put his atop Edme's, and they were made paw fast under the rising constellations of the stumbling wolf, Beezar, from the old world and that of the Narwhale from the new, the Distant Blue.

"Look, Edme, another constellation rises."

"The Sark!" Edme exclaimed. "It's the memory jug of the Sark!" Twelve stars sparkled in the night. It was as if the constellation had risen to catch the memory of this moment when two wolves from across the shoals of time were finally brought together and made paw fast again. The two turned and headed back to the brigade, to their new clan of motley creatures, whom they would lead into the world of the Distant Blue.

CHAPTER EIGHTEEN

THE ABDUCTION OF ABBAN

WHILE EDME AND FAOLAN BECAME paw fast under the first shine of a new moon, Abban crept down to the base of a pillar. He had a hankering for some capelin, and his mum was sleeping soundly. He often crept out when she was asleep. Ever since he had fallen into the sea, she didn't let him out of her sight. But tonight, with a sudden and very thick blanket of ice fog rolling in over the bridge, it was easy to sneak out. Not even the Whistler and Mhairie, the wolves on watch, saw him scramble down the gentle slope of the ice pillars.

Abban's mother just didn't understand that falling into the sea had been the best thing that had ever happened to him. At first it was scary. He'd never felt so alone in his life; the sea had seemed to expand into an awesome and terrifying infinity. But once he had begun to plunge into its depths and the creatures came near, the terror receded. He and this salt world were kindred and well suited, better suited, he thought, than he had ever been to the Outermost, and he felt closer kin to these creatures that swam gently around him than to his father. *Why is that?* he often wondered. *And why have I come back speaking so oddly?*

When the words were still in his mind, they sounded nothing like the way they came out when he spoke them aloud. Something got twisted up in his head when he tried to speak aloud. And everyone thought he was half *cag mag*. But it simply was not so.

He peered down into the water. Would he see the mysterious brinicles? The ones the fish called the teeth of death? They formed beneath the sea ice, reaching down from the frozen ceiling and sometimes touching the floor of the ocean. They were twisted into stunningly beautiful shapes resembling plumes of frozen smoke, but they could be deadly, especially to bottom-dwelling creatures such as starfish and sea urchins, which would freeze to death on contact with them. The brinicles were the coldest things on earth, their glacial edges as lethal as the sharpest battle claws a Rogue smith could make.

Dumpster and Dumpkin had just placed half a dozen

capelin neatly at Abban's paws when Dumpkin let loose with an earsplitting buzzing noise. Abban jumped, but not soon enough. He felt fangs lock on to his hackles, and his feet were swept off the ice. He smelled a scent he knew too well. The scent of Heep!

But it was not his father who was carrying him. His father was beside him. Abban had been snatched by Bevan, an enormous wolf, the largest of the rout that Heep led.

"Don't make a sound, or else Bevan will slice right through your neck to the life vein. The ice will turn red with your worthless blood."

Worthless, you say. Does this make sense?
To go to such a great expense
If I have no worth
Then why on earth?

"Shut up," Heep roared, but his jagged howl was drowned out by the clamoring of the puffins. Scores of them sounded the grating squawks that were their alarm calls.

On top of the bridge, the Whistler and Banja looked down at the mass of puffins that had gathered. Some were floating on the water lapping the pillar's base. Others were flying overhead.

"What in the name of the Dim World is going on?" the Whistler howled. It was a high, piercing howl that split the raucous cacophony of the puffins. Dumpette alighted and stumbled toward them. By this time, several other wolves, including Mhairie and Dearlea, had roused themselves.

"It's . . . it's . . . it's . . . it's . . ." Dumpette was stammering madly, her chunky orange beak clattering away, creating yet another layer of noise. Suddenly, there was a pealing mournful howl. Caila raced into their midst. "He's gone!"

"That's what I've been trying to say all along, He . . . is . . . gone! They took him!"

"Who's gone? Who took what?" the Whistler said.

Caila screamed, "Abban. He's gone!" She began howling, "Abban, where are you? Abban!"

The Whistler crouched down and growled at Dumpette. "Look at me, Dumpette. Calm your gizzard or whatever you puffins have in there. Think! What happened? What did you see? Just take it one step at a time."

"Steps? But we don't walk very well. We fly better and are great swimmers! But steps?"

Ay yi yi! These creatures are so literal, the Whistler thought. It was going to drive him *cag mag.* He did not want to get angry. After all, these birds had fed them. But something had to be done to bring Dumpette to her senses, if indeed she had any. A pup had been nabbed. With each minute, the situation was growing worse.

The Whistler walked stiff legged toward the puffin until he was just inches away. He skewed his body into one of a wolf's most aggressive postures. He held his tail straight out, his hips twisted into an angle as if he were about to leap onto this bird who was a fraction of his size. He shoved his ears forward and peeled back his lips, then emitted a fearsome growl that sounded as if it came from the Dim World.

Dumpette quivered and swallowed several times. She shut her clownish eyes until they were just thin black elliptical marks in the pools of white feathers on either side of her beak.

"All right. Are you ready?" she said, and then she blinked at the Whistler.

Of course I'm ready! the Whistler wanted to scream but repressed the urge. "Yes, now just begin at the beginning."

"The beginning? That's before the middle or the end, right?"

Great Lupus, thought the Whistler. He was ready to bite the dumb bird's head off. He nodded.

"Well, Abban was just eating some fish we had brought him. Minding his own fish business. You know how it is when one minds fish business. You just eat them and —"

"Just go on. What happened?"

"All of a sudden, these two wolves came around from behind the pillar and just snatched him. One wolf did. One really big wolf."

"Was one wolf yellow?"

"Yes, but not the big one."

Caila gave a yelp of horror. "I knew Heep would come back. I knew it! Just knew it!" She collapsed on the ground, sobbing. Banja rushed to soothe her.

"How did these wolves get onto the pillar without us seeing them?" Mhairie asked. "I don't understand it."

"Nor do I," the Whistler said. He turned to Dumpette for an explanation.

"Ice tongues," Dumpette said, clacking her beak shut.

"Ice tongues? There weren't any ice tongues when we made camp on the bridge tonight. We checked."

"They can form quickly in this weather. One could have broken off from a pillar base and the current could have pushed it along faster than you were traveling."

"But how — ?"

"Simple!" Dumpette said. "It's a long narrow sheet of ice. The currents carry it here, and it mates."

"Mates?"

"Yep, couples up with the Ice Bridge and makes a connection, not just a single connection. They often make two. It depends on the current and the eddies."

"So," the Whistler said, "if I understand this correctly, the ice tongue broke off from some pillar and got swirled around and reattached again near us. If Heep was on it, that would be perfect for sneaking up and snatching a pup."

"Exactly!" Dumpette exclaimed. "Here's how." Dumpette began dragging her beak across the ice, and Whistler blinked. This dumb puffin was actually making a crude drawing. "Here's the bridge. We're here." She made an X on the bridge. "The ice sheet broke off from a pillar base and got swirled around to here." She made another X. Dumpette had begun to speak so fast that the wolves only caught a few of the words: "attachment point," "westerly," and "pillar."

The wolves stared at Dumpette in disbelief. It was as

if she had experienced a sudden infusion of brains into that ridiculous head of hers.

"What are you staring at?" Dumpette asked.

"You!" Dearlea exclaimed. "I mean, please don't take offense, but you're talking so sensibly, so . . . so intelligently."

"Oh, no offense," Dumpette said sweetly. "When I get going, I really go! That's the way we all are. Puffins are a little slow off the starting mark, but hey! When we're off, we're really off!"

"Do you have any idea where they could have taken Abban?"

"Well, that's the problem. Ice tongues are much more complicated than they look, especially at this time of year."

"Why this time of year?"

"It's getting to be spring. With the sea ice breaking up and more water . . . well, you see how water washes in and carves out deep caves and tunnels into the tongue? They've probably hidden him away in some cave. There could be dozens of them."

"Oh, no!" Caila wailed.

CHAPTER NINETEEN

"THIS IS MY STORY"

AS FAOLAN AND EDME MADE their way back to where they had left the brigade, they spotted more rocks similar to the one where Faolan had found Edme sleeping. Scattered about them were what looked like a collection of small leaves.

"What in the world is this?" Edme crouched down and examined the leaves closely with her single eye.

"Leaves?" Faolan asked, crouching next to her. "But there are no trees. And look at these things. They're fuzzy."

"These aren't leaves. Not at all," Edme replied. "I think, Faolan — I think some of these things are cocoons."

"Cocoons? You mean for butterflies or moths?"

"Yes, I believe so. In the Beyond, such creatures were rare. But look! One of them is moving just a bit."

They watched for several minutes until suddenly the cocoon began to split. They sat transfixed as the split lengthened and the tip of something poked out. A few other cocoons began to jiggle a bit and soon were showing signs of splitting. But Faolan and Edme kept their eyes on the first cocoon. They sensed that they were witnessing a great drama, a drama of life like none they had ever seen.

"Look! It's a wing tip if I ever saw one!" Edme said with great excitement. The cocoon seemed to heave and nearly rolled over. A moth staggered out.

"At last!" The creature sighed. "At last!"

"At last?" Faolan said. He and Edme were astonished. The creature had spoken, and they understood it. But why was the creature saying "at last"? And they were not sure how they understood the language the creature was speaking, for it was not exactly Old Wolf.

"Yes. I'll say it again. At last!"

The creature's wings, which seconds before had been crumpled and damp, were beginning to dry and spread out. They were a soft golden hue. Down the middle of its back between its wings was a column of black dots. "Do you want to know why I said 'at last'?" Faolan and Edme both nodded. "It has taken me fourteen winters to get to this point in my life. To fly."

"Fourteen winters!" Edme cried.

The moth spread its wings and began to flutter off into the air, shimmering in a sliver of moonlight like a gold coin. She did a few loops in the air and then settled down. "How's that for a beginner?"

"Lovely!" Edme exclaimed.

"I don't understand any of this. You've waited fourteen winters to fly?" Faolan asked.

"Yes," the moth replied, and turned to look over at a half dozen other cocoons that had begun to split. "It takes time," she whispered. One of the fuzzy creatures began to move. An orange-and-black-banded caterpillar oozed across the ice.

"Bindle, that you?" the moth asked.

"Yep. Five more winters to go."

"And then you'll fly?" Edme asked the caterpillar whom the moth had addressed as Bindle.

"I better!"

"This is very strange," Edme said.

"Weird," agreed another caterpillar who had just begun to move.

"All right, have to say good-bye. Gotta start eating now. Our season is short. Guess we won't see you again, Bells." Bindle, the first caterpillar, directed his comment to the moth.

"Why not?" Edme asked, and immediately sensed

that perhaps she shouldn't have. "Oh, I'm sorry. I didn't mean to ask you such a personal question."

"No need for apology," the moth answered pleasantly. "It's not personal at all. It's simply the way we are. I'll die before the summer even starts."

Edme and Faolan both blinked. They had never heard any creature speak so calmly, almost cheerfully, about their impending death.

"You don't sound very sad or upset," Faolan ventured.

"Why ever should I be? I get to fly! At last I get to fly! Fourteen winters and I am finally me!"

"Me, too," another voice squeaked out from one of the recently split cocoons.

"Oh, Tris. It's you! I thought you were just in your thirteenth winter."

"No. Same age as you." The moth's wings were as damp and wrinkled as Bells's had been a few minutes before. "Let me just dry out and get the kinks out of my wings, and I'll join you for a flight."

"Explain all this to us," Edme said looking about, for now there seemed to be many more cocoons than they had first noticed, and a small area of the Ice Bridge was covered with either wriggling caterpillar bodies or flashes of gold as the moths lifted into the dark.

"Well, this is my story." Bells paused. "Our story," she said, nodding at Tris. "We are creatures who in one sense have many lives." Faolan and Edme exchanged glances. "I daresay we are much older than you by many winters. We began as eggs laid by our moth parents," Bells continued. "And then we turned into very tiny woolly bears." She nodded at Bindle.

"Woolly bears?" Faolan asked.

"Yes, because we're fuzzy. Every summer, we woolly bear caterpillars must eat. But the summers are so short we can't ever eat enough for . . . for . . ." the moth began to stammer slightly. "For the big change. Eat enough to grow wings, to have the energy to fly. See, Bindle here can't do it yet. He needs to eat for a few more summers to get the energy."

"And during the winter? What will he do?"

"Freeze. Freeze solid." Bindle seemed to yawn as he said this, but it was hard to tell for his mouth was so tiny.

"Yes. That's what I did for thirteen winters," Bells said. "At the beginning of autumn, my heart would slow and then stop completely by the second autumn moon."

"Stop?" Edme said in a hushed voice.

"Yes, stop. And then my gut would freeze, and next my blood and everything else."

"But why aren't you dead?" Faolan asked.

"I'm not sure. There is something in our blood that protects us from being damaged forever, even when we freeze. However, in our last autumn, our fourteenth, we weave a cocoon from the hairs of our own body — the woolly bears' hairs and the silk."

"Silk?" Faolan and Edme both asked, for they had never heard the word.

"Yes, silk. It's . . . it's . . . oh, how to explain! Something like your fur, I suppose. Now that I think of it, what kind of a furry creature are you?"

"Wolves," Faolan replied. "You've never seen one?"

"Not in my caterpillar days," Bells replied. "But as I was saying, we make silk and, with the silk and the hair, weave cocoons. And so we are sheltered, and finally fat enough, and can at last grow our wings. This spot on the Ice Bridge is a good place to roost for autumns and winters. These rocks," she said, lofting herself into a fluttery flight above them, "are ideal. They give us protection for overwintering, and when the warm weather comes, they harbor the heat so we can hatch out or thaw out and resume our lives. Which means eating a lot for the woolly bears and flying a lot for me!"

"Look, the caterpillars are moving away to the west."

"Yes, back to a good food source. Indeed, we can crawl quite fast as caterpillars. But as you might imagine, flying is even faster."

"And where will you fly?" Edme asked.

"West, the Great West."

"You mean the Distant Blue?" Faolan asked.

"Is that what you call it — the Distant Blue?" Bells asked.

"Yes."

"Curious." She said this word softly and fluttered right up to Faolan's muzzle. "Perhaps I can show you the way. It's not far."

"It's not?" Both Edme and Faolan leaped to their feet.

"How far is not far?" Edme asked.

"Oh, just a bit beyond that star." Bells flew straight up and seemed to hover directly beneath it.

"Kilyric!" Faolan cried out.

CHAPTER TWENTY

SILENCE AND ICE

AS FAOLAN AND EDME APPROACHED camp, the air was filled with the clack of puffins' beaks.

"They sound absolutely hysterical," Edme said. "What is going on?"

Dearlea came charging toward them. "Heep! Heep has taken Abban."

"What? How?" Faolan was dumbfounded.

"You see that ice tongue?" Dearlea said.

Edme followed Dearlea's gaze. "It wasn't here when we left."

"No, it was. The ice fog was so thick we couldn't see it."

"Where did they take him?" Faolan asked, hackles bristling.

Mhairie now came up. "It's a mess, Faolan. We don't

know where he is. Those ice tongues are riddled with caves and tunnels. And Caila and Banja already took off. There was simply no stopping Caila."

Mhairie paused. Her eyes filled with tears. She gulped. "He'll kill her!"

"No! We'll kill him before he can touch her. Where are the eagles? Where are Zanouche and Eelon?" Faolan said.

"Out scouring the ice tongue for any sign of Heep and his rout."

Katria and Airmead raced up with Gwynneth.

"Airmead and I have been talking. We have a strategy."

Faolan wheeled around to her. "What is it?"

Airmead spoke. "Long ago, in the time of the War of the Ember, the MacNamaras were led by the Namara in a formation called a *slink melf*."

"*Slink melf* — what does that mean?" asked the Whistler.

Few of the other wolves had ever heard the phrase before, but Faolan and Edme had heard of the formation. "It's a kind of *byrrgis*," Faolan replied.

Katria and Airmead exchanged glances.

"I suppose you could think of it as that," Katria said.

"Not really." Airmead shook her head. "In truth, it's an assassination squad, and we often swim. That was how it was done during the War of the Ember."

"Swim?" The other wolves were flabbergasted.

"I'll explain quickly, for we mustn't lose any time," Airmead said. "As you know, the MacNamaras lived the closest to water, the Bittersea, of any of the clans. In the time of the War of the Ember, the first action occurred in the northern kingdoms. Nyra and the Pure Ones were trying their talons at some horrendous *nachtmagen*. Some of the Pure Ones had flown to the Ice Palace near the H'rathghar glacier."

"*Nachtmagen!*" Edme exclaimed.

Gwynneth *wilfed*. There had been no owl in the Hoolian kingdoms more dreaded than Nyra, mother of Coryn.

"Yes, dark magic that some ancient owls once practiced. In any case, they thought they were safe there. But they weren't. The Namara got wind of them before any of the Guardian Owls of the Great Tree on the island of Hoole. So she organized a *slink melf*. Two scores of wolves crossed the Bittersea, then swam across the Bay of Fangs to the Ice Palace."

"They swam that distance? In that cold water?" Mhairie asked.

"Indeed. We have been trained to swim since we live in such close proximity to the Bittersea," Katria explained.

Airmead continued, "The water is calm tonight. We can swim around the ice tongue. It won't be that hard."

"We should do it. We should do it now," Edme burst out.

The wolves all turned to her in amazement. Edme had been the most stubborn of all the creatures about staying on the bridge. They all assumed she was deathly afraid of the water.

Faolan was stunned. He walked up close to her. "You'll swim, Edme? You'll actually leave the bridge?"

Edme dropped her voice so low no one could hear her except Faolan.

"Faolan, I found what I needed to on the bridge. I know the place." She nodded but did not speak more for fear someone would hear her. But Faolan knew what she meant by "the place." It was the place of *cleave hwlyn*, the place where her first *gyre* had died nearly one thousand years before. "I am at peace now. I can leave the bridge. And I can swim better than you might imagine." There was an impish glint in her eye. "Let's go!"

When the last scrap of the moon slipped over the horizon into the Distant Blue and the world turned black, when the night was in its darkest phase and the constellations rose, the wolves and the two bears slid into the water. Myrr and Maudie, much to their consternation, were left behind with Gwynneth to watch over them.

Myrr watched as Edme swam away from the bridge toward the ice tongue. His anger at being left behind had receded. Instead he felt fear growing inside him. *What if she doesn't come back? What if something happens to her?* This was not the first time someone he loved had left him behind. This situation was different from the time his parents had turned their backs on him, but the feeling, the terror, was the same.

Airmead and Katria led the *slink melf* as they swam out and around the bend of the ice tongue. Bobbing silently in the breaking dawn were shimmering ice floes that had been sculpted by wind and storms into amazing shapes. Had their task not been such a deadly one, they would have perhaps taken time to read creatures into these shapes as they liked to do in clouds, to discover an elk or a crouching wolverine or a rearing grizzly. But they swam on, their tails lifted out of the water so as not to put a drag on their speed, their heads held high to avoid the splash of waves. Luckily, the water around the tongue was fairly flat, and the wind was low. Their first objective as they circumnavigated the ice tongue was to understand the geography of it. The structure was more intricate than they would have ever suspected when viewed from the top of the bridge. There were small inlets that narrowed into tapering channels and penetrated the ice. In these channels, numerous ice caves had formed, but the channels were so tight that the eagles with their broad wingspans could not fly through them.

They had surmised that Abban would not be found in one of the caves close to the water since the outclanners were deeply fearful of the sea. However, there were also tunnels in the ice that most likely wormed through to the top, and there could easily be caves in the tunnels. It was crucial that the wolves find a way into these tunnels from the bottom, from the water. And this was where they hoped Dumpette would be helpful. For with a wingspan much smaller than an eagle's, she could fly high up above the channels and scout. She could ascertain if there might be an entrance from above that Heep and his followers had used to sequester themselves, as well as poor Abban.

The wolves also kept an eye out for Caila and Banja. It had been foolish of those wolves to set out by themselves. Faolan understood that they had been desperate, but this was a situation in which pack mentality was needed. That mentality was at the core of the ethics of wolves. They worked together as a team, whether it was defending their territory or hunting.

As the morning grew brighter, the ice seemed to turn bluer. Edme glanced at Faolan. His silver head now seemed tinged in the blue light of the floes. There was such silence, too, as whatever wind that had blown seemed to expire in the ice maze they were swimming through. Silence and ice. That was all there was as they wended their way through the crystalline architecture of the ice tongue. Silence and ice.

CHAPTER TWENTY-ONE

ON THE TONGUE

RAGS CROUCHED DEEP IN A TUN-
nel, his belly aching with hunger. How had everything
gone so wrong? When he knew that he could not endure
another second in the rout, when the memory of the wolf
called the Sark began to seep into his dreams every time
he shut his eyes, he had finally decided to leave. He was
careful to stay behind the rout. There was no choice:
Faolan would have attacked instantly. They knew that
Heep's rout was behind them, looking for a chance to
strike, to reclaim Heep's mate, Aliac, and their son,
Abban. If Faolan had spotted him, Rags would have been
torn to pieces. He was in an untenable position on the
Ice Bridge.

He heard wolves above him on the tongue. Why were
they staying? He could not leave until they did. He could

only guess that it was still too foggy to find the way back to the Ice Bridge. For now he was virtually marooned on the tongue with the rout. How much longer could he last here? The ice tongue seemed bereft of any of the small rodents that had provided food for them, such as lemmings, voles, and the occasional fox. There was fish, of course, but fish meant getting close to the water. Rags's only consolation was that Heep and the rest were as hungry as he was. So why didn't they leave? Surely by now they could find the attachment, even if it was still foggy, and get back to the bridge where there was plenty of small game.

He thought about all this as he crouched in the tunnel. He managed to doze off briefly until an alien smell penetrated the air. He saw it. Four green slits slashing the darkness.

I've been found! He knew those eyes. Aliac! Rags began to tremble.

"Rags!" Caila growled. "Where is he? I'll tear your throat out." The wolf beside her gave a low snarl that seemed all the more frightening because of its softness.

"Aliac, what are you talking about?"

"My name is Caila, and I am talking about my son, Abban. They took him."

"Took him? I can't . . . I can't . . ."

"You can't what?" Banja snarled again and stepped close to Rags. She was a fearsome wolf, with heavily muscled legs. He knew in a flash she must have been a Watch wolf at the Ring of Sacred Volcanoes.

"I . . . I . . . I can't believe they took him. How?" Rags stammered.

"How doesn't matter. Where is he?"

For the first time, Rags felt a flicker of an emotion that was foreign to him and almost indescribable. It was a sense of decency. He stood up and lifted his tail slightly.

"I don't know where he is, Caila. I left the rout. I am a lone wolf now."

"You left the rout? You left Heep?"

"Yes, and now I am *kuliak*."

"*Kuliak?*" Banja repeated the word.

"Yes. A *kuliak* has been pronounced upon me for leaving."

"What does *kuliak* mean?" Banja asked.

"It's an outclanner word. It means cursed to death by the rout."

Banja sniffed. "Well, I would say to simply be an outclanner is curse enough! To be an outclanner and cursed by a rout is twice cursed and thus a positive thing. In my mind, you have been blessed. Yes, precisely. Twice cursed equals once blessed."

"Why did you leave?" Caila asked.

Rags sighed. "Because somewhere deep inside I felt a yearning for something I've never known, something decent, to live righteously and with honor."

"And yet you're here, still here." Caila's eyes narrowed.

"I'm trapped. I didn't know the ice tongue was forming. If I go ahead, I'll run into your group and be attacked instantly. If I go back, I'll find the rout and Heep. But now I know why they stayed. They've got Abban."

"Exactly. He was fishing. The child fears nothing about the sea. And the puffins bring him fish."

"And you set out to find him."

"Of course. I am his mother."

"But where are the rest?"

"They'll be coming," Banja said. "Faolan and Edme were scouting ahead when Abban was taken. But I can assure you they'll be coming."

Abban crouched in a tunnel nearby. It had all happened so fast. A thousand times in the brief hours since his capture he went over the details. Was there anything he could have done? Any way he could have reacted more quickly? Why hadn't he heard his father creeping up on the other side of the pillar? He had been very busy eating and right before that peering down into the sea, dreaming about all the lovely creatures he had seen and those mysterious and deadly brinicles.

I am too dreamy, thought Abban. But, oh, if he could have one of those brinicles now, he would stab his father in the heart and happily watch him die. He had heard his father talking about his mum. He had declared her *kuliak*. He didn't precisely know the meaning of the word, but he was sure it had something to do with murder, with killing his mum. Abban knew he had been taken to lure his mum to her death.

Elsewhere on the tongue of ice, Heep, Bevan, and three other wolves had their noses close to the ground, following a new scent. Or was it two? Heep was not quite sure. Scent tracking on ice was difficult, and he had noticed that since he had been driven out of the Beyond and into the Outermost, his sense of smell had worsened. Some had said you can't smell your own if you eat your own, and the Outermost wolves were no strangers to cannibalism. During the famine, they had attacked the dazed and *cag mag* Skaars wolves and fed on them. It had helped the outclanners survive.

The first time Heep saw Caila, she had been attacked at a Skaars circle and was bleeding. He had followed her bloodstained trail, fully intending to devour her. She would be easy prey, weakened from the loss of blood. But when he recognized her as the distinguished turning guard of the MacDuncan clan, he decided to spare her. To be a turning guard in such a powerful clan, one had to be truly a superb runner — fast, strong, and relentless in pursuit. She was too much of a treasure to kill for food. He decided instead to make her his mate.

Some treasure, he thought now. She had been docile enough at first, but soon after the Great Mending, when his tail was restored, something had turned in her. She became obstinate, always challenging him. The more he had wagged his tail, the more contrary she became. Then there was that last night. Just before they had come out of the strange cave on the edge of the Outermost, she had seized Abban, his only child, and sprung into the night. Heep had never seen a wolf run so fast. She was a blur, like a shooting star across the night.

Suddenly, a familiar scent prickled his nostrils. His hackles bristled. It was her, Aliac!

"I got something! I got something!" Heep was so excited his voice seemed almost strangled with a snarl. His marrow sizzled with vengeance.

Bevan came over, and he sniffed the ground.

"There are two scents. One might be hers," Bevan said.

"What do you mean might? It's Aliac."

"Yes, of course." Bevan laid back his ears, tucked his tail, and began to lower himself into the posture of submission.

"She's down there in that tunnel. Bevan, Krupp, go back and fetch the pup."

"Yes, sir," they both answered. And as they went, each knew something else but dared not say it to the other. There was a third scent — the scent of Rags. Had Heep really missed it? If so, it was an indication that he was not nearly the wolf he had once been. Each of the outclanners thought to himself, *Heep is vulnerable. I can take him down!* They dared not say it aloud, for each one had dreams of becoming the most powerful wolf in the new world that was drawing nearer all the time.

Meanwhile, the wolves and the cubs, led by Airmead and Katria, continued on their desperate swim. The *slink melf* had the same basic configuration of a *byrrgis*, and for the first time in many days, the wolves felt themselves back in a clan. It felt comfortable, despite the fact that they were swimming and not running.

A scent began to waft their way, and Katria, out in the lead, was the first to catch it.

She signaled to the wolves behind her as they had in a *byrrgis*, with the voiceless signs of flicked ears and tails. These subtle motions and gestures were dense with information.

Faolan passed on the signal to Dumpette, flying above. This was tense, for he was uncertain if the puffin could really keep the code for the signals in her head after her one flashing display of intelligence. Unlike the cubs, who had learned the code immediately, Katria had needed to go over it three times with Dumpette.

Faolan glanced at the cubs. They could hardly be called cubs anymore. They were huge and they were beautiful swimmers, along with possessing an extraordinary intelligence. He knew they missed their mother, Bronka, as much as he missed Thunderheart. He had vowed to try his best to be their protector, their big brother, their father. He and Edme, of course, had rescued Toby from the MacHeath wolves many seasons ago. But he had grown equally fond of Burney. How ironic that these two cubs, one of whom had been cubnapped himself, were now part of this vital effort to rescue Abban.

Of course, rescue was only one part of the mission. Heep and his followers had to die. If they were to live in peace in the Distant Blue, there could be no outclanners. Not a single one could be left on the Ice Bridge. They all had to die.

CHAPTER TWENTY-TWO

THE YIPS OF ABBAN

"COME ON, BOY!" BEVAN YANKED
Abban by his ear. "And none of that *cag' mag* talk of
yours."

So this is it, thought Abban. They didn't have to
tell him. He knew he was being set up as bait, that his
mother must be nearby. Bevan dragged him to where
Heep was standing on the tongue in the first light of the
graying sky.

"Start yipping," Heep snarled. Abban stared at his
father. He had such loathing for Heep. How could they be
of the same marrow? Abban clamped his mouth shut so
none of his nonsense words would tumble out.

His father stepped closer and grabbed him by the
muzzle. "Did you hear me, boy? Start yipping. Make
the milk yips. You want your mother's milk."

But I have been weaned! Abban wanted to say. He feared it would come out all wrong. *If I yip for milk, she'll know something is not right. She'll suspect a trick.* Then Abban realized he wanted nothing more than his mum to suspect a trick. And so he yipped.

In the tunnel of the ice tongue, Caila startled at the sound of the yip. "Abban!" she barked.

"No!" Banja growled, and stepped forward to block Caila's way. "It's a trap. He's weaned."

"I . . . I . . . know but . . ." And mysteriously she felt a sensation of milk stirring within her, although she had been long dry. "But I have to go to him!"

"It's a trap," Banja repeated.

"It is," Rags said. "The rout will be waiting for you. It's big. More wolves have joined since you left."

"I don't care how many there are! If it's a trap, we'll be trapped together. Abban and I will die together on this tongue of ice." Caila closed her eyes and imagined the star ladder to the Cave of Souls. She was slipping back into an old dream, a deadly dream. The dream that had lured her toward death when she imagined Skaarsgard, the keeper of the ladder, descending to fetch her and guide them to the Cave of Souls. In her mind's eye, she saw an image of herself and her dear pup climbing the ladder together.

The air in the tunnel was laced with the yips of Abban, and Caila was weakening. There was no way Banja could hold her back. No way.

Caila burst out of the tunnel onto the ice tongue and saw him. A pathetic figure in the first rosy light of the dawn.

"Don't, Mum. It's a trap! Run! Run!" Abban howled.

Bevan grabbed Abban's haunches. Heep locked his jaws around his son's hackles as Abban twisted furiously in his grip. Behind them, more than a dozen outclanners had scrambled out of ice holes that pocked the bridge.

And then several things happened at once. Eelon and Zanouche both plummeted from the sky. Eelon aimed directly for Bevan's face, and there was a flurry of feathers and a terrible screech. Then Heep saw it — Bevan's eyeball rolling across the ice. In his horror, he let the pup loose. Five wolves led by Katria burst from a hole in the ice tongue, followed by two grizzlies, no longer in their cubhood but almost full grown.

Rags and Banja leaped into the fray. The rest of Heep's rout charged down the tongue, which was turning slick with melt water in the early morning sun. The wolves were slipping, struggling to get enough purchase to even fight, but the bears with their longer claws and heavier weight were invulnerable. Digging in with their hind claws and swinging their forepaws, they batted at the rout wolves as if they were flies on a summer night. There was a terrible howl as a dusky wolf skidded off the ice and dropped like a stone into the water. He bobbed up once, still alive but too frightened to even move a paw, before the sea closed over him. The water dimpled as he sank, as if to mark his grave.

Heep recovered his wits and was steadily fighting his way toward Abban, who was perilously near the edge of the ice tongue and in danger of falling into the sea. But this seemed to make the pup all the more fearless.

"Come now! Come get me!" He danced on the slippery edge of the tongue. Heep trembled with fear, the image of what had just happened to his first lieutenant seared on his mind. Drool hung in long silvery threads from his mouth.

Sensing the rout's terror of water, Faolan and Edme had tried to move the outclanners close to the edge, where, like owls going yeep, they suffered bone freeze and could be easily shoved in. The Whistler made a bold charge at two wolves that went flying off into the sea, but lost his own grip and followed them. It was not a long fall, and he was not hurt. The wolves in the water looked at him in astonishment as he began to swim. "Help us! Help us!" But he turned away, ignoring their pleas, and paddled back to the tongue, where he clambered out ready to rejoin the fray.

Abban taunted his father from the edge of the tongue.

"I'll get you . . . you worthless —" Heep screeched at his son. That's when Caila charged him, clamping her teeth on his tail. Bevan howled and leaped toward Abban, but Zanouche plunged from above and scooped up the pup in her talons. Bevan skidded to a halt, then pivoted to attack Caila.

"Get her off my tail! Save my tail!"

But it was too late. There was a ripping sound, and the furry plume sailed out across the ice tongue, caught in a sudden gust of wind. Red drops trailed behind it like the particles from a bleeding comet.

Heep went mad in his fury. He charged the closest wolf, Banja, who had raced over to help Caila. His fangs tore a huge gaping slash in her throat.

The ice tongue was now streaked with red. The other

rout wolves had proven no real match for those led in this skirmish by Airmead and Katria. The *slink melf* had killed eight and driven back the remaining ones. Edme had just delivered a fatal bite to a she-wolf when Banja was attacked. She dashed to Banja's side, but she knew as soon as she looked that Heep had delivered a mortal blow. Banja's vital life-pumping artery was ripped open, and blood gurgled from her nose. She tried to speak.

"Don't speak, Banja," Edme soothed. "I remember my promise, our promise. Gwynneth and I vowed to take care of Maudie. We will. We will." She felt a sob swelling in her throat, and her voice cracked as she tried to continue. "I'll . . . I'll raise her as if she were my own — I promise you . . . I . . ." Edme could hardly get the words out, she was so wrecked with the shock and the horror of the blood gushing from Banja's neck. "I'll never let her forget you. Never ever!"

Banja's eyes rolled into the back of her head. There were three words she wanted to say. *Please, Lupus,* she thought. *Just these three.* "I . . . trust . . . you . . . ," she managed. The three words cracked in her throat like jagged pieces of ice, but they would never melt.

Tears streamed from Edme's eye. These last words would linger forever in her mind and forever astonish her.

"Trust" was the last word anyone had ever expected to hear from Banja when she had been a wolf at the Watch. Giving birth had transformed a once embittered and jealous creature who had never trusted anyone. Edme bent close to the dying wolf's head, gently lifted Banja's earflap with her tongue, and whispered, "I know, dear Banja. Gwynneth and I will not fail." She paused to dash a tear from her eye, then she repeated, "We shall not fail." But by this time, Banja was gone.

A soft breeze like a whisper blew across the ice, and Edme could feel Banja's spirit fleeing. She looked down at what was left behind. *It's just a pelt*, she thought, *a pelt and some bones. Discarded, too heavy to climb the star ladder.* "Skaars speed you," she whispered softly, and the wind seemed to swallow her words.

CHAPTER TWENTY-THREE

"How Will She Find Her Way?"

"IT'S A NICE CLEAR DAY," GWYN-neth said, blinking into the morning light. "We'll see them as soon as they round that bend. Zanouche said they wouldn't be long."

Gwynneth stood on the bridge and looked toward the ice tongue. Beside her stood Myrr, Maudie, and Abban. Zanouche had reported that when she had swooped in and rescued Abban, the battle was going well. So far no one had been wounded, but they had delivered many wounds to Heep's rout and at least eight rout wolves, possibly nine, were dead.

"They have no discipline," sniffed Gwynneth.

"I think I see them! I think I see them," Myrr said, jumping up and down. They turned their heads to look. The two bears were in the lead, and following in their wake, the heads of the wolves bobbed into focus. Gwynneth squinted. It was hard for her to see quite that far and especially around the rather large heads of the bears. But she thought she spotted Airmead's bright white head and next to her Katria. They were coming closer. *And, yes, there's Faolan, Edme, Mhairie, Dearlea, and the Whistler, but . . .*

"Where's Mum?" Maudie's voice had grown small. "Where is she?"

Gwynneth felt dread clench her gizzard. She extended a wing and patted the little pup. "I'm sure she'll be coming, dear." She hated herself, but what else was she supposed to say?

"She's not there, Gwynneth!" There was a terrible ache in the pup's voice. They watched as Edme swam furiously ahead.

"Can we go down to meet them?" Myrr asked.

"No, dear, I think it's best we wait right here," Gwynneth answered.

"But where's my mum?" Maudie's question was broken by a sob. And before Gwynneth could stop her, Maudie raced down the sloping edge that led to the pillar.

Edme saw the pup as soon as she clambered onto the base.

"Where's my mummy, Auntie Edme?" Maudie asked.

Gwynneth alighted beside her and spread her wing over the pup's shoulders. She tilted her head and looked at Edme, then shook it slightly as if willing Edme's next words to be untrue.

"Maudie, dear, your mother . . ." Her voice broke. She stopped and took a deep breath. "Your mother," she tried again. "Your mother was a very brave wolf, but she died on the ice tongue." She paused. "I am so sorry." Edme nearly bit her own tongue. Her words sounded so weak, so stupid.

Maudie blinked several times. Death was an idea, a notion that was simply too large, too complicated, too unspeakable for her to comprehend. "Oh, no!" Maudie howled. The other wolves had climbed out of the sea with Toby and Burney. They all gathered around the little pup, licking her as she wept the bitterest and saltiest tears ever shed on the Ice Bridge.

"What will I do? What will I do?" she wailed.

Edme crouched down close to her. "Gwynneth and I will take care of you. And Faolan. Faolan and I are now paw fast."

Gwynneth blinked at this news, but said nothing. It was not as if it was unexpected, really. They all had sensed that Faolan and Edme were linked.

"We will raise you," Edme continued. "We will comfort you. We will feed you."

"You have no milk!" Maudie said stubbornly and stomped her foot.

"You were almost weaned, dear," Gwynneth said.

"No, I wasn't! Mum still fed me at night. She did! She did!" Maudie turned on Gwynneth. "And what do you know about milk? Owl mums don't have milk. They feed their babies worms and disgusting stuff. What will I do?" She began to wail again.

"Maudie," Toby said as he and his brother approached her. "We lost our mum, too."

"It's awful," Burney said. "Just awful."

"Burney's right," Toby said. "There's nothing worse. B — b — but we're here and everyone loves us . . . I . . . I think almost as much as our mum did."

"Not almost," Burney said. "Just as much!"

"We do!" all of the creatures of the brigade chorused.

Maudie began to gulp in between her sobs.

"Listen to me, Maudie," Edme said gently but firmly. "Here is what you're going to do." There was something in the tone of Edme's voice that made Maudie stop her wailing.

"What?" she said, her voice seething with resentment.

"Tonight when the darkness comes we shall begin the *glaffling* of the *morriah*." The dark, portentous words brought Maudie up short.

"What is that?" she asked, her voice trembling.

"It is our grieving howls for your mother, Banja, a wolf of the Watch and a wolf of great courage. A wolf who was a wonderful mother and most of all a wolf we had learned to trust. Do you understand, dear?"

Maudie nodded slowly. "I think so," she whispered.

"Each night, beginning tomorrow, we shall wail the *morriah*, to send her on her way to the star ladder. You know about the star ladder, don't you?"

"Mum told me it's where wolves go when they have . . . have . . ." She couldn't finish.

"Yes, that's it, Maudie. And we shall look for her *lochin* every night. You know what a *lochin* is?"

"The spirit mist of my mum." Maudie gulped. "How will she find her way if there's no star ladder here?"

All the wolves' eyes flashed green. Maudie had voiced the dreadful question in all their minds. The star ladder disappeared for the three winter moons and then reappeared with the first spring moon. For wolves of the Beyond, winter was a terrible time to die, for they must wait through the long hard snow moons — that of the First Frost, those of the hunger moons until the Moon of the Cracking Ice, when the first stars in the first rung of the star ladder returned. It was a desolate time in which the spirit was caught in a strange limbo between earth and heaven, between the spot of *cleave hwlyn* and the Cave of Souls. The homeless spirit was lost and stumbling, not unlike Beezar the blind wolf. But eventually spring came, and the spirit could ascend.

Now, on the Ice Bridge, betwixt the old world and the new, the only constellation the wolves had seen and recognized was that of Beezar. There had been no trace of the star ladder or Skaarsgard since they could remember. There were new constellations, but they had left the old ones behind them. And if this was so, what would they do for a heaven?

"Faith!" Faolan said, addressing all of their muffled fears. "Don't you recall that old *skreeleen* story of the toothless chieftain who had slipped from his pelt and leaped to the first rung of the star ladder? Suddenly, he fell off back to the ground, and became the chieftain from the land of the Long Cold who led the first clan on the

Ice March. He came from the Distant Blue, so there must be a star ladder there. We must have faith."

Faolan crouched down directly in front of Maudie. "The star ladder will be there. If not tonight, another night."

"But will she be all right?" Maudie tipped her head up. "If the stars are so few?"

"Yes, of course," Edme said as Gwynneth stroked Maudie's pelt with the downiest part of her wing.

"But if the star ladder comes back — maybe she could fall off it like the old chieftain did? Maybe?"

"I don't think so," Edme replied. "We must howl to help her mount that star ladder. When your mum was a wolf of the Watch, she was a brilliant jumper, really one of the best. On her Watch, she did the most spectacular leaps to guard the volcanoes. So beautiful and effortless."

"She was as graceful as an owl when she was air-borne," Gwynneth said.

"Really?" Maudie asked.

"Really!" the entire brigade of creatures chorused.

Later that morning, the battle-weary creatures sought out snow snugs to rest just for a while. Maudie fell instantly asleep alongside Myrr, who was tucked in between Faolan and Edme. Gwynneth perched on a small ice outcropping and kept an eye on the pups. Caila, too, slept nearby with Abban pressed next to her. Mhairie and Dearlea together stood the watch.

CHAPTER TWENTY-FOUR

THE *MORRIAH*

BY THAT EVENING, THE MOON had thickened into what the wolves called a true moon claw. Beezar was rising and so was the Narwhale. The brigade had traveled only a short distance that day, as they were exhausted from the clash with the rout the previous night. They had reached the place where the bridge forked and had gathered to begin the *morriah*. No one wanted to say anything, but it was hard not to forget that there were still nine, possibly ten, outclanners somewhere behind them. It was a distraction during a ceremony that was supposed to be one of deep reflection on Banja's life and her spirit journey on the star ladder.

Maudie stood between Edme and Gwynneth. "How does the ceremony start?" she asked. At just that moment, a note swooped into the night. It blossomed, sustained and beautiful, above them in the sky like a constellation composed of music rather than stars. It seemed to sparkle in the deep blue dome that hung over the Ice Bridge. There was only one throat that could have issued that note — the Whistler's. This was the summoning call that began every *morriah*.

Then a more delicate, fragile strain was heard. Dearlea threw back her head and howled the first verse:

Oh, Banja, brave Watch wolf and mother
The ladder waits for you beyond the dawn
In the west in a night to come
You will find the first rung
Oh, Skaarsgard, may you help her
Climb this ladder to the star trail
Stay beside her, and guide her
To the Cave where souls rest
Oh, Banja, your pup is safe
She is cherished. We keep her dear
She will not wander,
By our marrow we'll protect her
And keep her near
Never forsake her
Let no one break her,

Or ever take her.
Your precious gift —
To her we shall be true
And bring her to the Distant Blue.

As Dearlea concluded, they remained still for a long time, many looking down at their paws, weeping quiet tears. But the Whistler looked at Dearlea. He was mesmerized by not just the loveliness of her voice, but the words she had summoned from some place deep within her. She was a poet and true *skreeleen.*

He felt an unfamiliar twitch in his marrow. It was not simply a profound admiration, but something more.

Could this be love? he wondered. For an instant, he wondered who could love a wolf with a twisted throat, but then he remembered that his throat had grown whole during the Great Mending. Still, he had been a gnaw wolf and she had been raised in the Carreg Gaer of the MacDuncan clan. There was a world of difference between them. The Whistler knew he should not be thinking of such things at this time. He should be thinking of poor Banja and her orphaned pup, Maudie. He noticed now that while the others had kept their eyes down, Maudie's were fastened on the sky above.

"What's that, Edme?" the pup asked.

"What's what, dear?" Edme looked up and caught the flutter of gold that had caught Maudie's attention. "Oh my goodness, it's Bells."

"Bells?" the Whistler said.

Bells alighted on the ice. Her wings cast a shadow several times larger than their actual size.

"My sorrows, little one," she addressed Maudie. "From one who has lived fourteen winters, your mother's early death seems so shocking."

"Thank you," Maudie said softly. She was almost afraid to breathe for fear she might blow the beautiful creature away. Maudie crouched down so she could see her more closely. "I never thought anything so tiny could speak," Maudie said.

"You learn a lot in fourteen years, even though our waking hours are short — summer short, as we say."

"You are lovely. What are those spots on your back?"

"The marks of the woolly bear caterpillar that I once was."

"Oh," Maudie said simply.

"I am here to guide you — all of you. We must begin tonight, for spring is here and summer will follow and the Ice Bridge becomes dangerous. We must take the north fork, the one where you, Edme, and you, Faolan, first found me. Do you have enough strength? I know the day has been long and hard and sad."

"But you are so tiny," Maudie said. "If you have enough strength, surely we do. We are so much bigger." Her eyes opened wide, and all the wolves looked at her in wonder. The simple words that she had spoken to the golden moth had inspired them and sent a pulse through their hearts that quickened their marrow. The animals rose together.

"We must follow the north fork," Bells repeated. "It's the safest way."

The brigade was more than pleased to hear this, because in addition to their worries about Heep and his remaining rout, there was another concern — that of cracking ice. As Dumpette had warned them, with spring, small pieces of the bridge had begun to break off. The breaks were augured by an eerie creaking sound, which scarred the days and seemed to lessen as night came on. But this night, they had heard more than a few, and then splashes as the pieces of ice fell off. Gwynneth, with her superior hearing, was able to sense these creaks almost before they began far down in the ice. To the others, they sounded like creaks, plain and simple. But for Gwynneth, some were rasps, some groans, and sometimes she would report that the ice was "complaining" and guide them around the source of the complaint.

The brigade was getting closer after all these moons, closer to the Distant Blue. Bells flew just above Maudie's head, and every now and then, Maudie would look up and catch sight of the fluttering gold creature. Sometimes in a buffeting gust, a bit of gold powder would drift down and sprinkle the ice, and once the gold fell on the tip of Maud's nose.

"What's this?" Maudie asked.

"Don't worry," Bells said. "Just a bit of dust from my wing scales."

"Can you still fly?"

"Oh, yes, but by the time we get to the bridge's end, my wings will be bare. Some consider it good luck to be dusted by moth wing scales."

"I hope so," Maudie said, although on this day, lucky was the last thing she felt.

The golden moth flickering in the night became a guide for Gwynneth. Like a tiny glowing lantern, Bells offered a bright beacon for her to follow. But on the second night of their travels, Gwynneth became aware of a strange new phenomenon. Owls, particularly Masked Owls, who were members of the Barn Owl family, were renowned for their superior hearing. With unevenly placed ear slits, one slightly higher than the other, an owl like Gwynneth could capture the smallest sounds. And by expanding or contracting the muscles of her facial disk, she could actually guide these sounds directly into her ears, scooping them up from the night. It was possible for Masked Owls to detect the heartbeat of a mouse on a forest floor far below or the sound of lemmings scratching nests beneath the ice. But now Gwynneth realized she was able to hear a sound many times smaller than even the heart of the tiniest mouse. She was hearing the wing beats of this minuscule moth who was half the weight of a dry leaf.

Gwynneth was delighted. For it seemed that as her eyesight had dwindled, her hearing had sharpened. That was how she picked up the sounds of the cracking ice, and now she could hear snow melting! That would have seemed impossible three moons ago. Still, Gwynneth was glad that her eyesight had not deteriorated any further. She was not entirely blind, thank Glaux! With her newly sharpened hearing, she was navigating better than she had ever hoped.

For five nights, the wolves traveled hard, resting for only the shortest periods of time. During the day, the Distant Blue had become more distinct. The eagles flew out on regular surveillance flights to scour the bridge for any sign of Heep and the remnants of his rout, but so far they had seen none. It was possible that the Ice Bridge had become so soft that the rout could quickly dig itself in and hide at the first sign of the eagles. It was unnerving to see no sign of them.

The moon claw had doubled in size and soon had swollen to a half moon, tilting slightly lopsided into the night. Each night, Beezar rose higher and the star of Kilyric burned brighter. Sometimes they imagined that they could see more than just the loom of the Distant Blue, but the continent's true coastline.

"Yes, soon the Distant Blue!" Bells exclaimed. Her wings had grown duller in the night, and she shed more scales whenever they encountered contrary winds. But she seemed no less energetic. The creatures that she guided marveled at her strength.

On the sixth night, the moon had fattened to cast a bright silver light on the ground where Gwynneth had paused for a short sleep. A noise penetrated her dreams. The wind was up, but threading through it was a distinct sound — the footfalls of wolves.

Gwynneth jerked awake and shreed the alarm call. But before the brigade could rally, the shadow of a tail-less wolf spread across the ground.

"Take the pups to a safe hole!" Faolan howled.

"You're too late!" snarled Heep.

CHAPTER TWENTY-FIVE

A FORTRESS IN THE SEA

SIXTEEN OUTCLANNERS, A NUM-
ber far exceeding the worst fears of Faolan and his friends,
encircled them. Caila was stiff legged with fear in the
middle of the snarling wolves, with Abban crouching by
her side.

"You're not going to succeed," Faolan growled.

"Wait and see," Heep snarled.

Edme stalked toward Heep, Maudie gripping her fur.

"Don't go! Don't go!" Myrr shook so hard he thought
his legs would buckle. *I can't lose her. She's my only mum! I
can share her with Maud, but I can't lose her.*

It was as if a fire had been ignited in his marrow.
Myrr bolted from their snug and hurled himself as hard as
he could at Heep's rump, still sore and bloodstained from
the loss of his tail. Heep yowled as if his tail were being
torn off all over again.

It was just the distraction the brigade needed. The Whistler charged the wolf next to Heep. The eagles plunged from the sky and began to fight on the ground, slashing at the outclanners with their powerful talons. Mhairie and Dearlea ran as a *byrrgis*, attacking the largest of the outclanners. Mhairie began the classic press of an outflanker, then the blood of a seasoned turning guard began to boil in Caila and she leaped forward. The mother and two daughters were now a *byrrgis* of three — Caila resuming her position as turning guard, Mhairie as outflanker, and Dearlea passing signals between her mum and sister.

Caila was running full out when from the corner of her eye she saw another wolf slide into the *byrrgis* position. Rags! But he was working with them. He had bitten into the hindquarters of an outclanner wolf, and they wrestled him to the ground.

"I'm running with you!" Rags growled. And the *byrrgis* of three was now four.

Then Edme gave a terrible howl. Two wolves led by Heep pounced on Faolan, and there was a hideous crack.

His spine! They broke his spine!

Fangs hung over Faolan's neck, ready to rip into his life-giving artery, when the sound of a crack whipped across the night again. It was so resounding that it seemed to shake the stars.

"Urskadamus!" Faolan swore, and sprung to his feet.

Edme nearly fainted from relief when she saw Faolan jump up. *It was the ice!* she thought jubilantly. But the bridge shifted under her feet, and Edme's marrow seized up. The blind wolf was stumbling over the western horizon. The bridge was breaking, crashing!

Gwynneth plunged out of the night to grab Maud just before the ice gave way, and the wolves, noble and savage alike, plummeted toward the water. Myrr clung to Caila and Abban as they fell.

"ABBAN!" Caila shrieked. But the seas seemed to part to embrace the pup. He paddled with his paws and sculled with his tail. He saw the slightly distorted image of his father, paws churning frantically as he tried to propel his head above water.

Abban heard a voice in a watery language. "You're swimming, lad. You're swimming. You can do it!"

It was Old Tooth. The narwhale whisked by Abban. "I've got business ahead." He pointed with his tusk toward Heep. Abban watched transfixed as Old Tooth flashed by him, his sword bright in the moonlit water.

There was no sound. Nothing. That was what Abban

would always remember — the immense quiet of that moment. There was only a thick plume of blood in the water and Heep impaled on Old Tooth's tusk.

"The leopard seals will be coming. I'll feed this creature to them. But the seals might go wild. Get well behind me." There were other voices in the night. Abban took one last peek below the water, and the first voice he heard when he surfaced was Faolan's.

"Edme?"

"Here!"

"Whistler?"

"Here!"

Abban knew instantly what this was even though he had never heard it before, having been born in the Outermost. It was a *byrrgis* roll call.

"Mhairie?"

"Here!"

"Dearlea?"

"Here!"

"Caila?"

"Here! But where is . . . ?"

"Abban?"

"Here!" he called out. "I'm here, Mum. I am here!"

"Airmead?"

"Here!"

"Katria?"

"Here!"

"Burney and Toby?"

"Here!"

"And here!"

Gwynneth hooted from above, "I'm here with Maudie!"

"And we are here with Myrr," Eelon called down.

Caila swam up to Abban. "Abban, thank Lupus!"

Abban opened his mouth to speak, and to his shock, his words didn't tangle into rhymes. "I'm here, Mum, and he's dead. Heep is dead. He'll never bother us again."

Caila howled out. Rags was flailing in the water, and she surged over to him. "Rags! Help me with Rags!" she called.

Mhairie and Dearlea quickly paddled up so they surrounded him.

"Don't panic," Dearlea said. "We'll help you." They pressed against him, buoying him up.

It was as if the Frozen Sea had melted entirely. There was an infinity of water, and the ice floes had shrunk to nothing. Abban swam over to his mother and sisters, who were giving Rags an emergency swimming lesson.

"Don't worry," the pup said. "It will all be fine. They'll help us. They will, I promise. The whales will come."

Old Tooth surfaced, issuing an indecipherable series of hoots and whistles that Abban seemed to understand. He turned around and spoke to Faolan.

"There's danger! Leopard seals and sharks are coming."

Faolan looked about. He saw a score of tusks swimming nearby. One broke off and headed for the desperate wolf Rags as the fin of a shark sliced through the water.

"The fortress, Faolan. The fortress against the wind. The narwhales!" Edme howled.

She didn't have to explain. The narwhales, too, seemed to understand. They gathered in a tight circle around the brigade and directed a series of clicks, trills, and whistles at Abban.

"What are they saying?" Faolan asked.

"They say grab hold of their fins and climb onto their backs," Abban replied.

And so they did. Caila and Abban helped Rags mount Old Tooth. The whales were huge, and it was easy for the animals to ride in twos and even threes on their long backs. The water around them churned, and the tusks of three dozen narwhales scraped at the night. Caila saw a pink froth on the water.

"That's blood, isn't it, Abban?" she asked quietly.

"It's Heep's blood. Sharks are tearing him apart. They might be hungry for more, but we're safe. We're safe, Mum."

Just outside the barricade of the narwhales, they saw the slashing fins of great sharks and the occasional grunt of a ferocious leopard seal as it surfaced for breath. The sharks' mouths revealed gleaming rows of sharp white teeth, and the fangs of the leopard seals flashed like daggers in the moonlight. But the narwhales swam on calmly, deliberately, and with a speed not matched by any of the predators who attempted to circle them. With a flick of their powerful tails or a sudden jab of their tusks, they drove off any shark or leopard seal instantly.

From the back of the narwhale on which she and Faolan rode, Edme looked up into the night sky. Maud was safe in Gwynneth's strong talons, and directly ahead of Gwynneth, Edme spotted the soft glimmer of Bells's wings nearly bereft of their dust.

"Can you see her, Gwynneth?" Maudie asked.

"A bit, dear. But more important, I can hear her. Every little flutter of her wings."

There was a large, hollow watery sound as if the sea had gulped. All the creatures turned their heads. The remnants of the Ice Bridge were riding low, with fragments breaking through the green water. Every animal in the brigade experienced a strange wistfulness. The bridge had sustained them for so long, and now it was being devoured by the sea.

Abban's gaze lingered until at last he turned around to face the open sea before them.

CHAPTER TWENTY-SIX

THE DISTANT BLUE
DRAWS NEAR

THE WIND THAT HAD BEEN ON
their noses died down, and the whales began to swim at a
breathtaking speed. The Distant Blue seemed so close,
but it was not until the following night, under an almost
fullshine moon, that Eelon spotted the coastline of the
new continent. On the breeze came a wonderful verdant
smell — the fragrance of grass. All through the night, the
travelers' hearts soared as they drew closer and closer to
this new world.

"New world." The two words sang in their heads. No
one slept, no one shut their eyes for a single second. As
the sky lightened just before the true dawn, they spied the
headlands. The Distant Blue was here and it was not blue
at all but green and tranquil before their eyes.

They all drank in the sight of this new land, and no
one more so than Dearlea. She looked back one last time

at the open sea before the whales swam into the shallower waters of a bay. Behind them, the wreckage of the Ice Bridge rose from the water like the fractured bones of some monstrous mythical sea creature. And behind the bridge, far in the east, where the sky would grow dim and night would fall as the sun rose here in this new world, a nightmare faded. The Long Cold was over. The march across the Ice Bridge would soon become distant memory, too, but Dearlea was determined that it would not fade entirely. She knew that forgetting was for the dead and memory was for the living. The quiet desperation she had felt when Mhairie had said that there was not time for *skree* circles came back to her and so did the words she had spoken to her sister. *Don't you see, Mhairie, if we don't keep telling the stories, we shall forget them. And if we forget them, our marrow will leak away, our clan marrow will vanish.*

Now was not the time to forget. Now was the time to remember. *Memory,* Dearlea thought, *is the life-pumping artery, the blood in that artery. Memory is the sinew, the muscle that stretches back to the Beyond and before the Beyond. Have we not come full circle?* she wondered. *Now is not the time to forget.*

She felt a quiet despair, for there was song deep within her desperate to get out. Lupus, she would not die with the song inside her!

Her mother, who rode next to her on another nar-whale's back with Abban, turned toward her and howled, "Sing, Dearlea! Sing! You are a *skreeleen*. The first in this new world."

So Dearlea threw back her head and sang.

> *And out of that dark place we fled*
> *That broken land so scarred and dead*
> *Our hopes our dreams forever gone.*
> *Then did we follow this wolf so bold*
> *To this place that did unfold*
> *As if lost in mists of time*
> *It was the Distant Blue*
> *A new world sublime.*

> *On a bridge of ice we walked and walked*
> *We now give thanks to Lupus, to Glaux,*
> *To Ursus and gods not known,*
> *And to whales who carried us*
> *The last way*
> *To here in our new home.*

The other creatures began to join in. The wolves howled, and from Toby's and Burney's deep chests came sonorous roars that stirred Faolan's heart. Dearlea was so right to sing, to remind them of what they had left behind.

They had called their final shelter on the other side of the Frozen Sea the Last Den. Now they were clambering ashore onto a crescent of beach that was bare of snow or ice, but with an embankment above the high-tide line that looked rife with shelters. Here they would find their First Den.

Abban had turned back and entered the water. He was swimming toward Old Tooth.

Faolan barked, "We must join Abban and thank Old Tooth." So the creatures swam toward the pod of circling whales.

"The tide is going out," Abban said. "You must hurry, for they cannot stay here long."

The blood of Heep still stained Old Tooth's tusk, but Abban swam up to the spot just between the narwhale's brow and his blowhole and licked the mottled gray skin with his tongue. He made some odd sounds, sounds that a wolf had never uttered. And Old Tooth closed his eyes contently and seemed pleased.

"We don't speak their language," Mhairie said.

"It doesn't matter," Abban replied. "Lick them just where I did. It's a way of saying thanks."

So each wolf and the two bears swam to the narwhales that had transported them and began to lick just where Abban had. The whales were soon flopping their tails happily, churning up the water.

Abban laughed. "Old Tooth says you better stop thanking them or none will want to leave and the tide will be gone."

So the wolves and the two bears scampered out of the bay and onto the beach. Abban ran up to the highest promontory he could find, an outcropping of rock that overhung the bay. He watched the narwhales as they swam from the bay toward the distant horizon. He wept the tears of *wilig*, which were the special happy-sad tears that wolves sometimes cried. They did not sting as much as other tears, and some said they had an amber color.

There were no other kinds of tears to weep on this occasion. For Abban knew that he had within his one life really lived two — that of a wolf and that of a sea creature. It seemed somewhat miraculous that for a few brief and shimmering moments he had been granted these two lives, two worlds. Blessed he was, but how had it ever come to pass? How had he fallen into the immensity of the sea and found creatures so dear? How had he come to understand their language? Now it was time to say good-bye to the sea and these creatures who had saved his life and taken the life of Heep, who had tormented him since the day Abban was born.

Caila came up beside him. She seemed to read his mind. "May he go to the Dim World and never find his tail." She nuzzled Abban's withers. "Come now, let's go down and join the others. The sun is setting. We should find a den."

"Not yet, Mum. I want to stay up here for a while, until dusk falls. I can still see their tails and their tusks. I want to remember them always. They look so noble, so valiant, like the guardians you told me about."

"You mean the owls? The Guardians of Ga'Hoole?" Dearlea padded up to them.

"Yes. You have to tell us what you know. We cannot forget them." Dearlea nodded her head toward the east. "They are so far away, but we cannot forget them — the owls, the Guardians of Ga'Hoole."

"I can remember." Gwynneth alighted, and she cocked her head toward the east as if listening for a story to be brought on the wind.

"Once upon a time, a very long time ago, there was an order of knightly owls from a kingdom called Ga'Hoole, who would rise up into the blackness and perform noble deeds. They spoke no words but true ones. Their purpose was to right all wrongs, to make strong the weak, mend the broken, vanquish the proud, and make powerless the savage. With hearts sublime, they took flight." The four wolves and the owl perched on the promontory for a long time. Just as dusk began to fall, the time the owls called First Lavender, the last of the whales' fluked tails dipped over the horizon.

Edme came seeking the four wolves and Gwynneth. "Come down. Bells is leaving us," she said quietly. They turned their backs to the sea. Abban was the last to follow, and before he left, he turned his head once more but the narwhales were gone. Not a trace of the Ice Bridge could be seen.

When they arrived on the beach, they found the animals standing in a circle, peering down. In the center of the circle, Maud was crouched close to the ground with a bit of gold dust on her muzzle. Edme entered the circle, settled next to Maud, and began stroking the pup's flank with her paw. Gwynneth had alighted on Maud's other side. Maud did not lift her eyes from Bells. Every now and then, one of Bells's wings fluttered a tiny bit, but her wings were no longer gold. They were completely transparent. Gwynneth could hear her infinitesimally small heartbeat grow slower and slower.

"We're here, Bells," Maud said in a whisper as gentle as the brush of a moth's wings. Maud studied her intently. So this was *cleave hwlyn*. This was what happened to her mother, but on a battlefield of cold and bloodied ice with savage wolves. If her mother had to die, why couldn't it have been on this quiet beach? There was no blood, no savage shrieks, but only the sand and sky now with the stars about to break out.

"I know you are, Maud." Bells's voice was very faint.

Maud wanted to say something more, something important. But she couldn't think of anything. Then some words spoken to her on the night of her own mother's death came back. The words spoken by Bells. "My sorrows" — she paused — "golden one."

"I gave you my last gold," Bells said cheerfully. "And there is no cause for sorrow. Remember, fourteen years I have lived. So many years, so many lives. From caterpillar to moth. I have flown! What could be more . . . magical?" And then no more. "Magical" was the last word Bells uttered before she died.

Gwynneth put a wing around Maud's shoulder, and

Edme ran her muzzle through her hackles in a comforting gesture.

"Don't worry. I'm all right," Maud said, rising to her feet. "Look! Look!"

"Great Lupus!" the Whistler howled. "It's the star ladder."

And indeed Molgith, the first star in the ladder, was just appearing on the horizon.

"And the mist! The mist!" Maud cried. "The mist of Mum."

"Banja's *lochin*!" Edme cried out. "It jumps the rungs of the star ladder just as she jumped at the Watch. I told you your mum was a beautiful jumper."

"But look just ahead of her," Maud howled with wild delight. There was a tiny flash of gold fluttering in the new night.

"Bells!" they all cried out.

"Bells leads her," Maudie cried, and her voice broke. Edme came up to lick the tears from her face.

"Aah, you're weeping *wilig* tears. True *wiligs* they are. See, they're amber!"

Epilogue

THE WOLVES, THE BEARS, THE Masked Owl, and the eagles slept peacefully that night. But between the time that Beezar stumbled out of sight over the far horizon and the morning star appeared, before the first rosy hues of the dawn, Faolan left the den. He wanted to travel away from the coast a few leagues and see what kind of land this Distant Blue was. The long grasses were sprinkled with wildflowers that he had never seen. But there was meat. He sensed it, and soon they would have to find the meat trail.

For months, they had eaten nothing but fish and small, nearly bloodless rodents. He knew there was life abroad in this land. He could almost smell the blood of the big hooved animals. Bigger than caribou. Big as moose. He found a track. He could tell by the way the hooves sank in that the track had been made by a large creature. Brush was broken. A herd had come charging through. From some of the branches, long, thick clumps of coarse fur waved in the breeze like banners. He picked up a scent. A word came to him, a word he hadn't heard in a thousand years. "Bison." His heart beat. *Yes, huge herds of bison that would thunder across the plains here.*

Faolan was on a rise now. Below him was a narrow green valley. He looked across the valley, and he saw something moving down its center, flowing like a river. It was not bison; these creatures were not nearly as large. Their fur was not shaggy, but they had sweeping manes and, flagging out behind them, long tails. He heard a whinnying sound. On a promontory just ahead was a horse.

Yes, "horse"! That was the word. He knew that word. The animal was creamy white, but when it turned its head, Faolan was shocked to see that the creature's face was scarred as if it had run through fire. There was no fur, and the skin crinkled up in ugly ridges. The horse regarded him.

You're back.

And so I am, replied Faolan.

The horse suddenly reared up and pawed the air with its hooves. Then it whinnied loudly, *The Star Wolf is back!*

AUTHOR'S NOTE

THEY SAY WRITING IS A SOLITARY profession. It is not, however, as solitary as one might imagine. Voices, figures, and images from the past always haunt me as I write. It is time to acknowledge some of those sources that inspired parts of this book. Abban's fall into the sea owes a great debt to Herman Melville's character Pip in *Moby-Dick*, who came back mad from his plunge into the depths of the ocean. Dearlea's song on pages 109–110 was directly inspired by Bob Dylan's song "A Hard Rain's A-Gonna Fall." I am particularly indebted in terms of images to the fantastic BBC television documentary *Frozen Planet*. The cinematographers' stunning footage of the polar regions of the earth are indelible in my mind's eye.